Deep-Fried Twinkies
Life's Outtakes - Year 14

52 Humorous and Inspirational Short Stories

By
Daris Howard

A collection of stories, humorous anecdotes, thoughts, and tidbits of wisdom from the newspaper column *Life's Outtakes*.

Publishing Inspiration

Deep-Fried Twinkies

Life's Outtakes - Year 14

52 Humorous and Inspirational Short Stories

By

Daris W. Howard

A collection of stories, humorous anecdotes, thoughts, and tidbits of wisdom from the newspaper column *Life's Outtakes*.

ISBN-10: 1-62986-024-7
ISBN-13: 978-1-62986-024-4

www.publishinginspiration.com

Publishing Date: April 4, 2022

Publishing Inspiration LLC

Table of Contents

Dear Reader,

People often ask me if my stories are true. Though I must admit that I tend to take a bit of literary license in my writing, each story is based on an actual event. Sometimes the stranger stories are the ones that are stretched the least. As people often say, truth is stranger than fiction.

I also want to note that some of the names have been changed to protect the anonymity of the individuals.

Daris Howard

Moose Troubles

Our community has a moose problem. This time of year, moose start to move into our yards, eating fruit off our trees and vegetables from our gardens. Oh, they do it the rest of the year, too, but it is most prevalent in the fall. That is why a bunch of the men gathered around before church to share stories.

"How about you, Daris?" one of the others asked. "Have you had any problems with moose this year?"

"Not as much this year as in the past," I replied. "I had a mother and a calf come early in the spring. The mother left after busting up my trees. But the yearling she had with her was too sick to follow."

"What did you do about it?" someone asked.

"My wife called the Fish and Game Department and asked them to come remove it," I answered. "We didn't even want to chase it or anything for fear it would be too much for it."

"Did the Fish and Game Department send someone out?" another person asked.

"Yes, the officer came the next morning and asked if she could look around. You wouldn't believe what she found."

"A whole herd of moose had destroyed your whole orchard and garden," someone joked.

"Actually, she found the sick yearling had wandered into my open shop and died there. The Fish and Game officer said it was completely tick-infested, too."

Some of the guys grimaced at the thought of a tick-infested animal dying in my shop.

"The Fish and Game people came out the morning after that, dragged it out of my shop, and carted it away," I said.

"Maybe that is why no more moose have come around your place," one of the men said. "They don't want to catch the overabundance of ticks the other moose left you."

Just about that time, Cyrus hobbled in, leaning hard on his cane. He moved slowly toward where we were.

One of the men turned to him. "Cyrus, I understand you have had some moose problems recently?"

"I sure have," Cyrus replied. "There is one big bull moose that thinks he owns my property. He has eaten almost every apple on every apple tree I own."

"Have you done anything about it?" another man asked.

"Well, I decided I had had enough. So I got out my pellet gun, thinking I would give him a sting without causing any permanent damage. I thought that would be sufficient to drive him away and at least leave me a few apples for myself."

"Did the pellet gun work?" someone asked.

Cyrus shook his head. "It only made him mad. I fired a few rounds, and he started to move away, so I followed. But then, he changed his mind and turned and chased me."

"You're still here, so you must have beat him to the house," someone said.

"Did I ever," Cyrus replied. "If I had run like that in my college days, I would have set a world record."

Cyrus then turned and hobbled slowly into the chapel. We all stared after him.

Then Samuel said, "And thus we see that even a moose can be the source of a miracle."

A Blessing in Disguise

This time of year, as students head back to school, my mind often turns to football. I loved sports, but due to the amount of work on the farm, my father had a rule that we could only be in one sport each year. My brothers and I traded turns being in sports and doing the chores. But since I was one of the youngest in the family, during my sophomore year I had no one to do the chores while I was in wrestling. That meant I had to do the chores anyway. When one of the coaches asked me to come out for football my junior year, my father decided he'd let me as long as I kept good grades and still did the chores.

"But there is one problem," he said. "We might not always have anything available for you to drive for the practices. Your brother has first option to use the old car for college."

The car issue wouldn't be too much of a problem once school started and practice was after school. But football practice started weeks ahead of the first day of class. I talked to my brother about letting me use the car, but he wasn't keen on the idea, even when he wasn't using it. I considered driving the hay truck or a tractor the four miles to town, but I was sure my teammates would tease me. Then one evening, after hauling hay all day, I rode my bicycle to the usual swimming hole to meet my friends, and I realized I did have transportation if I wanted it.

When the first day of football practice came, I left early and rode my bike. Practice the first weeks was called the inferno. I had not experienced it before. And when practice was over, even though I was in better shape than most of my teammates, I could still hardly drag myself to the locker room. The thought of riding my bike the four miles home about killed me. When my teammates saw my transportation, they laughed and wished me luck as they climbed into their cars.

By the time I got home, my mind was reeling with the feeling of unfairness that I didn't have a car to drive. But when I raised the issue with my father, he simply said, "If you truly want to be good in sports, having to bike to and from practice will just make you that much better."

The next day, I could hardly get out of bed, but my muscles eventually loosened up. By the time I rode to practice, I felt better. But by the time practice was over, I was even more tired than I had been the previous day. This went on for a few days, and I even considered dropping out of football. Then things began to change. I found the soreness easing up, and riding home was getting easier. I started pushing myself harder on the ride home. Soon I was riding it in around fifteen minutes, about a fourth of what it took the first night after practice when I had to stop and rest. I also found I was recovering faster.

In practice, I wasn't the best player, but the longer the practices went, the more I dominated in my area. I had been forced by my wrestling coach to run an extra couple of miles after everyone else quit, and I experienced the advantage that gave me. This bike riding forced me to do something similar for football.

When the first game came, I played offense the whole game. And toward the end of the game, as everyone was getting tired, the coach also put me in to play defense. By the third game, I played offense the whole game, and I played defense most of the game. The coach then added me to special teams, and from then on, I was seldom off of the field during the rest of the season.

One day, after a tough fought game, Coach pulled me aside. "Howard, I want to know something. I want to know how you can keep going at the pace you do?"

I smiled as I replied. "I've learned that doing just a little more, after everyone else is done, especially when you think you have nothing left, pays big dividends."

That was when I really realized how grateful I was that I didn't have a car to drive to practice like everyone else.

The Auction

Dean was a church leader, and his congregation needed to raise some money. So, he and his two assistants decided to have an auction. The people of the community seemed excited about the idea. They started to gather anything they felt was of value to the designated area behind the church.

On the day of the auction, the women of the community went all-out baking their most delicious desserts. Dean's wife made a beautiful three-layered chocolate cake. She covered it with chocolate frosting and decorated it like a pinwheel using M&M's. Dean's mouth watered just looking at it.

Just an hour before the auction, Dean got a call. He was disappointed to learn there were some problems where he worked, and he had to come in. He hoped to go in after the auction, but the situation necessitated immediate attention. He knew it meant he would miss the auction.

Dean's children were disappointed that their father couldn't come to the auction with them. Dean felt he was letting them down, but he especially felt he was letting his wife down because she had put a lot of work into helping organize the auction and in making her cake. He decided that he had to do something to show her he desired to be there.

He called his first congregational assistant, but all he got was an answering machine. Dean left a message telling his assistant to bid on the cake his wife had made.

"Bid as high as you need to go to get it for me, and I will pay you back," Dean said.

As Dean headed to work, he got thinking that his first assistant might not be able to make it to the auction because of the work he did, so Dean pulled out his cell phone and called his second assistant. When Dean's second assistant answered, Dean explained the situation.

"I want you to buy my wife's cake for me," Dean said. "Bid whatever amount needed to get it, and I will pay you back."

The man agreed to do so, and Dean went to work feeling better. When he finished taking care of problems at work, he returned home. The auction was over, and his family was already there.

"How did the auction go?" Dean asked.

"Really well," his wife answered. "We took in a lot of money. But the strangest sale item was my cake."

"How so?" Dean asked.

"Well, most of the food items sold for less than twenty-five dollars. But your two assistants kept bidding on my cake until it sold for five-hundred dollars. Then, strangely, the winner gave it to me to bring home, telling me to give it to you."

Dean gasped. He hadn't realized what he was doing in calling both assistants. He found out which one had won the bidding, and then Dean drove to the man's house and paid the five-hundred dollars for the cake. When Dean returned home, he explained to his wife what he had done.

Dean then ceremoniously called the family together. He placed the beautiful cake in the middle of the kitchen table. "Tonight, after we have finished our family bedtime routine, we are going to each have a piece of your mother's five-hundred-dollar cake."

After they finished their evening family activities, everyone trooped into the kitchen to share the cake. But as they came through the door, they were in for a disappointment. Their little dog was on the table, covered in chocolate, standing in the midst of the crumbs of what was left of the cake.

So, Dean never even got to taste the most expensive cake he had ever bought.

The Cello

It was only the third day of the school year, and Stephen came in late to math, the last class of the day. He was huffing and puffing as he lugged in a cello in a case that was heavier than the cello itself.

"Do you play the cello?" Mr. Davidson, the teacher, asked.

"Yes," Stephen replied. "I'm sorry I'm late. I hope you won't mark me tardy. It's a long way from the orchestra room, and it's impossible to hurry with something this big."

"Couldn't you just leave it in the orchestra room and get it after school?" a girl asked.

Stephen shook his head. "I normally would, but I have a cello lesson right after school, and I don't have time to get back to the orchestra room and make it to my lesson on time. So I had to run get it and bring it here so I can leave immediately after class is over."

"Why did you choose to play the cello?" a boy asked

"I love the sound of the cello the most of all instruments," Stephen replied.

"It would have been easier to choose something like a flute," the boy said. "You could haul a flute around with no trouble."

The students started teasing Stephen about his choice in instruments and how big it was. Stephen just smiled and took the good-natured ribbing. But it seemed to annoy Mr. Davidson.

"All right, everyone," Mr. Davidson said. "I, too, think that the cello is one of the best sounding instruments. In fact, I like it enough that I am not only going to forgo Stephen's tardy, but I am going to give him five extra bonus points for the day for his good taste and for his diligence in practicing and taking lessons."

A girl pulled a clarinet from her backpack. "How about bonus points for a clarinet? I practice diligently and take lessons, too."

"I might consider a few points, but hauling around a clarinet does not compare in dedication to a cello," Mr. Davidson said.

"I used to play the cello," Sally said. "Can I get an extra five points, too?"

"You used to play it?" Mr. Davidson said. "Why did you stop?"

"I quit," Sally replied. "It was too hard to haul around and practice."

"Quitting just because it was hard should be a negative five points, not a bonus," Mr. Davidson said.

"Did you ever play an instrument, Mr. Davidson?" one of the students asked.

Mr. Davidson nodded. "It just so happens that I love the cello, as well. When I was your age, I practiced it for an hour every night."

"Do you still play?" Stephen asked excitedly.

"No," Mr. Davidson replied. "I must admit that I wasn't the most talented musician, and my family begged me to stop practicing."

"So you quit, too?" Sally asked with a snicker.

Mr. Davidson turned to her. "I didn't quit. It is true, like I said, that my family begged me to stop, but I didn't quit."

"So what happened that you don't play anymore?" Sally asked.

"When I continued to practice, despite my family's pleas, my cello disappeared, and I never saw it again."

And then Mr. Davidson said in final, "That's why, lucky for you, I teach math and not music."

When Will We Ever Use This?

We were only in the first week of class when Evan asked something that would become the norm for him through much of the semester. We had just finished looking at some ideas on using math to make decisions in life when he asked, "When will we ever use this?"

I explained that the goal of this class, Math in the Real World, was to give the students lots of tools that would help them make the best decisions possible. I told him the first lessons were just laying down the steps that would be the framework for making those decisions.

From then on, there was hardly a class period when Evan didn't ask the same question. I feel it is essential for students to understand the value of what they are learning, but with Evan, it almost seemed like he would ask without thinking for himself. It was more of a habit.

He asked the question when we talked about making a budget and using it to make decisions about how to best utilize resources. He asked it when we went over Excel functions and how they could be used in different monetary issues. He even asked the question when we looked at the growth of investments in a retirement plan.

One day I was sure the discussion I had prepared would finally be such that even Evan wouldn't have to ask where he would use what he had learned. We started off the day by playing a game of The Price Is Right. The groups of students had to guess from gut feeling what they thought the total of a loan (interest plus principal) would be. The winning group got candy.

The loan was for one hundred and twenty thousand dollars, the interest rate was eight percent, and the length of the loan was thirty years. Most of the student groups guessed under two hundred thousand and were surprised to find out that the total would be around three hundred-seventeen thousand dollars. We then discussed ways the students had heard for reducing the amount of interest paid. One student said she had heard that if a person paid extra on each loan payment it would reduce the interest.

"But most people can't pay enough to make it worth it," a boy said.

"How much would you have to pay to make it worth it?" I asked.

He shrugged. "Probably about half of the normal payment," he replied.

We had found that the payment was around eight hundred and eighty dollars per month, so he suggested that to make any difference, a person would probably have to add about four hundred dollars on each payment.

"How much do you think most people could afford?" I asked.

The students couldn't seem to agree on a value, so I said, "How about fifty dollars? A married couple could go out for ice-cream on their dates instead of a full dinner and save that much a month."

I joked that I wasn't suggesting the husband not take his wife out, or the women would hate me. But I felt everyone could do fifty dollars. The students all agreed.

We plugged the numbers into the computer, and the students gasped at what it showed. It would save around forty-two thousand dollars in interest. The students then, as groups, tried some sample ideas with student loans, house loans, and car loans. We came back together as a full class to finalize the discussion and were just ending when Evan raised his hand.

When I called on him, he asked, "When will we ever use this?"

I stood there so stunned I couldn't speak. And before I could, Savannah, the girl next to him, did.

"Are you stupid or something?" she said to him. "The answer to your question is obvious." She then scooted her chair away from him. "Don't sit too close. I don't want it to rub off on me. And don't even consider asking me out."

I figured she answered him better than I could, so I didn't try.

And from then on, before he asked, Evan thought a little more for himself about how what he learned could be used.

A Bad Joke

When I was younger and had just graduated from college, we moved into a new area and into a new home. The church I was part of had decided to move all record-keeping to computers. The problem was that back then, very few people knew how to use a computer. So the congregational leader, who went by the title of "the bishop," asked if I would help enter the records into the computer.

One piece of this had to do with the donations the members of the congregation gave to the church. On Sunday afternoons, I worked with Henry to enter the data. He would read off the numbers, and I punched them in. This was before the days of the internet, so when we had checked and double-checked the numbers, we called into the church headquarters to report the data so the totals could be recorded there.

One day, the bishop came into where Henry and I were working. "I just got the phone bill," he said. "Do you know what's on it?"

"What?" Henry asked.

"There are a lot of calls to a dirty joke line," the bishop replied. "The calls are all made during the youth night meetings. Apparently, the youth are doing some things they shouldn't."

The next Sunday, the bishop talked about the issue to the congregation. He preached a little bit of fire and brimstone toward those who would use a church phone for inappropriate behavior and called on them to repent.

"Not only is it a disgrace to see these kinds of calls on our phone bill," he said. "But the numbers were 1-900 numbers and had charges both for long-distance and for a line charge. We are going to have some equipment put in so a person must have a code to make a long-distance call. That should take care of the problem."

Within a couple of weeks, the new equipment was installed. Henry and I were given a code we had to punch in so we could call in the weekly donation report.

Only a few weeks after the new equipment was installed, Henry and I had spent much of a Sunday afternoon recording everything. It was way past lunchtime, and we were both hungry and ready to be home with our families. It was Henry's turn to make the call, and my turn to watch and listen to verify he read the numbers correctly.

Henry dialed the number and punched in the security code. When the phone picked up on the other end, he smiled. He identified himself and the congregation he was calling from. Then he said, "I am ready to report the weekly donation information."

Suddenly, Henry blushed bright red. "Listen here," he said forcefully into the phone. "I don't want to hear any of that!"

Then he gasped. "Young lady, I want to talk to your supervisor!" He paused a minute and then said it again louder and with more force. Finally, he slammed the phone on the receiver.

Henry was shaking with anger as he turned to me. "That lady, and I use the term loosely, was telling me a dirty joke."

I laughed. "Henry, did you dial one eight-hundred, or did you dial one nine-hundred?"

Henry was not smiling as he replied. "As far as I know, I dialed one eight-hundred."

He was so shaken by everything that he wouldn't call again. So this time I dialed. A young lady answered and identified herself as a secretary at the church headquarters. She pleasantly recorded the information, and we hung up.

When the bishop stepped into the room, we told him what had happened. He laughed. "Well, I guess we know who was calling the dirty joke line."

Henry didn't think it was funny in the least. And when the phone bill came, it showed a nine-hundred number which, other than the nine, was the same as the church reporting number.

"Give me that bill," Henry said.

The bishop laughed. "We can pay for it."

"Not on your life," Henry said. "I don't want anyone saying I called a raunchy number and the church paid it."

He looked at the charge on the phone bill, plopped down five dollars, and said, "And keep the change."

Then he added, "And I don't want to hear another word spoken about this again."

Didn't Like Dogs

Marilyn didn't like dogs, and no one seemed to know why. Her children really wanted a dog, but she always said no. The children went to their dad and begged for a dog, so he approached his wife about it. Even he couldn't convince her that all children needed a dog.

"Why do you hate dogs so much?" he asked.

"When I was a teenager, my brother owned a Great Dane," she said. "He was always wandering off and causing problems."

"But that is no reason to hate all dogs," her husband replied. "Not all dogs run off and cause problems."

"It isn't just that he was always leaving. It was what he did."

By this time, the children had also gathered around. "What did your brother's dog do?" one of them asked.

Marilyn told them about how, when the dog would wander off, he would run all over, causing havoc. The dog would rummage through people's garbage cans, chase birds through muddy bogs, and all sorts of things. The neighbors were often annoyed at him because he would also terrorize the neighborhood cats, though he never hurt any of them. He seemed more intent on making friends with other animals, but his size made them all scared of him.

Marilyn said that when anyone noticed the dog had escaped from the backyard, it was all hands on deck, no matter what anyone was doing. One evening, just as Marilyn was ready to take the old Buick and head to town, her mother stopped her.

"Marilyn, Pixie is missing. We need you to help find him."

That was another thing that Marilyn hated about her brother's dog. Her brother had named the dog Pixie as a joke, knowing his Great Dane puppy would grow. The dog was huge, and going around calling out "Here, Pixie," only to have a dog the size of an ox come running, was more than a little embarrassing.

Marilyn tried to talk her way out of it, saying she really needed to go and didn't want to get dirty, but her mother insisted.

"You take the pickup truck, and if you find him, you can just have him jump in the back."

Marilyn finally agreed. She climbed into the front of the truck and drove around looking for the dog, hoping someone else would find him first. But luck was not to be on her side. She hadn't gone too far when she was sure she saw him. She considered acting like she hadn't, but she knew if she wanted to continue with her evening plans, she better help get him home.

She climbed from the pickup, leaving the door open so she could dash back in before he came. She walked toward where she thought he was, and sure enough, it was him. He had made friends with some pigs and was rolling in the mud with them.

She called Pixie, and when he saw her, his joy seemed to be unbounded. He came toward her at full speed. She turned and ran. And even in the high heels and the beautiful gown she was wearing, she outraced him to the pickup, jumped in, and slammed the door. She had expected Pixie to jump in the back like he always did, but instead, he flew through the window, right into her lap.

"It was to be my first high school dance," Marilyn said. "But even after I was cleaned up, I still smelled like a pigsty. Nor was I in the mood to go to the dance, anyway."

Eventually, the children and their father were able to prevail with Marilyn, and they got a dog.

It was a small one, and if Fluffy ever went missing, no one ever asked Marilyn to help find her.

Equal Respect

Rachel didn't like moving out west with her family, leaving their nice New England home. She was only eleven when they moved, and it was a long, arduous journey across the plains in the covered wagon. Her father worked hard and built a modest cabin, but three small rooms for twelve people made it more than a little crowded.

But what bothered Rachel most was how her father insisted they treat the Native Americans with respect. Most of the other settlers' children talked negatively about them, but Rachel didn't dare. More than once, her father had scolded her for her attitude. He was a religious man and insisted that everyone was equal in God's eyes.

"Rachel," he said, "if you treat others with respect, most people will return that respect to you, and your life will be better."

Another thing her father insisted on was that if any of the Native Americans came to their home and were hungry, they were fed. Rachel's father told her, "This was their land before we came. We are their guests, and they will be ours. If we have food, we will share it with them."

Rachel had hardly seen a week go by without a few Native Americans coming by. Usually, it was only Native American men traveling in hunting parties. But sometimes, there would be whole families, including mothers and children. When they came, Rachel's father encouraged Rachel and her siblings to make friends with the children, but Rachel would have none of it.

Rachel also despised having to share their food. There were some winters when they ran low and had to ration it. Rachel's mother was always cooking. Rachel's father mostly only grew wheat and potatoes because they gave the most food for the cultivated land. The Native Americans loved bread and potatoes. Rachel felt if they didn't have to share so much, her father might have food to sell, and then they could have other things that she liked better.

But above all, there was one Native American man that Rachel liked the least. It was not because he was mean or caused problems. It was because he always wore a skunk skin. The smell churned Rachel's stomach, and she would always go out and stay in the barn until he left. She called him Skunk Man, at least when her father wasn't listening. And try as she might, Rachel could not find any positive feelings toward Skunk Man.

Then, one day, after Skunk Man and the group he was with left, the family realized their youngest girl was gone. Rachel's little sister was only three, and Rachel was sure that Skunk Man must have taken her. Surely a child that small couldn't have gone far on her own.

Anger swelled in Rachel's heart. The family started to search, but Rachel was sure it would do no good. She was sure she knew where her little sister was. Rachel's older brother was dispatched to ride to the neighbors' houses, asking all he met for help in the search. Soon a large group gathered. They searched all day and much of the night, but to no avail.

Then, the next morning, Skunk Man and those with him were back. That made Rachel angry. Did they come back to admit what they had done? She could see by the neighbor's reactions that many of them felt the same way.

Skunk Man, using sign language, asked her father where the child had last been seen. Rachel's father took Skunk Man to the yard behind the house. Skunk Man got on his knees and looked carefully at the ground. Soon he and the men with him moved off in the direction of a small ravine. Others, including Rachel and her mother, followed. The Native Americans kept stopping and checking the ground and items around them, then continued on.

When they were less than a quarter-mile from the house, the men stopped at some bushes. They checked all around them, then

Skunk Man let out a loud yell. Suddenly, he started digging at an old badger hole, and the other men helped him. Eventually, Skunk Man slid face-first into the hole until only his feet were sticking out. Then he let out a yell from underground, and the other Native American men pulled him out. Tucked in Skunk Man's arms was Rachel's little sister. Her face was tear-stained, and she was a bit scratched up, but she was otherwise unhurt. When Skunk Man handed the child to her mother, Rachel watched her strong, brave mother break down and sob.

From then on, Skunk Man was one of Rachel's favorite people. She would smile when she saw him coming and invite him into their home. And she didn't even mind the skunk skin. At least, not too much.

God's Children

Rachel's family had moved west in the 1800s, along with many other pioneers. Life in the rugged land was challenging. Food was often scarce, as were many other essential items. But no matter how little they had as a family, Rachel's father always insisted that if Native Americans came and needed food, that their family would share with them. Rachel had at first detested this, but when her little sister was lost, some Native American men returned the favor and helped find her. That changed Rachel's attitude.

Still, in the winter, food was always in short supply, and feeding all those who came by put a strain on the family's supplies. With her and her siblings, plus their two parents, there were twelve in the family, and it was hard enough just to feed themselves. Sometimes, as the winter wore on, the food was rationed. Though the children usually had all they wanted, Rachel had seen her parents feign lack of hunger when she knew they had eaten almost nothing.

One fall, many Native Americans came through as they headed south for the winter. Rachel's father had worked hard to learn sign language, and he said the Native Americans told him it would be a hard winter. The family put away all the food they could, but it had been a tough year. Some June frosts had blackened the leaves of the potatoes, and the ones that did survive bore a small crop. Rachel saw their already limited food supply dwindling as they continued to feed the Native Americans. She questioned her father about it.

"Rachel," he said, "the Native Americans are God's children just as we are. If we help take care of God's children, He will help take care of us."

By November, winter set in, and the snow was deep and almost impassable. As Christmas approached, she heard her parents talking, and her father expressed concern that the food might not hold out until spring. She watched as her parents, especially her father, ate very little each day. If she ever mentioned it, he would pat his belly and say he could do with a little less weight. But she could see him growing thin, and she was concerned.

Rachel's father would go out hunting as much as he could, but the few times he did get anything, it was always only a small rabbit. He said he felt the animals had gone south for the winter, just like the Native Americans had.

When the storms were too much for her father to go hunting, he would whittle toys for the children for Christmas. Rachel's mother would sew dolls and knit clothes from the wool they had taken from their few sheep. Rachel had heard her father say that he might have to butcher the sheep. But he was concerned about what they would use for clothing if he did.

A couple of days before Christmas, Rachel heard her father say that come Christmas Eve, he would have no choice. He would have to butcher one of the sheep. But then, on the morning of December 24th, as her father was preparing for the task, Rachel saw someone approaching in the distance. As the person came closer, she could tell it wasn't one person, but a small group. It took until they were close for her to recognize a Native American man she called Skunk Man because of the skunk skin he always wore. But in this cold, he was wearing a thick buffalo hide instead.

Rachel ran to get her father, and he came to greet the men. They had two small horses with them, pulling loaded sleighs made from long, straight poles. As her father greeted the men, the family gathered around. Skunk Man signed, and Rachel's father signed back. Suddenly, Rachel saw tears rolling down her father's face.

He turned to his family. "Our Native American friends were concerned about how much food we shared with them when they came here. They were worried we wouldn't have enough left for ourselves. They have brought us two deer and half of a buffalo."

That Christmas, as they shared a feast with their Native American friends, Rachel realized that it was true that when you help take care of God's children, He helps take care of you.

Vacation Timing

I had been working on a doctorate for three years, with little time off. When I wasn't working on it, I was teaching, taking care of my family, or being a scoutmaster. I had already defended my dissertation, and my committee had passed it. I only had two more reviews to have it finalized. The current reviewer had had it for two weeks, but often they took months to go through it.

Our second youngest daughter had just gone away to college, and our youngest daughter was going with a tour group back east, so my wife, Donna, had a suggestion. "Since the girls are gone, why don't we take this week and go on a vacation?"

"The problem is that if my next dissertation reviewer comes back with fixes, I probably ought to do them right away," I replied.

"Do they insist that you do them immediately?" she asked.

"No, they never have," I replied. "They just tell me what they want changed, and then I work on it when I can. But I try to do it as soon as possible to speed up the process."

"What are the chances they will get back to you this week?" she asked.

I thought about that and considered the other reviews. Almost all of them had been more than three weeks, with some being quite a bit longer.

"We'd probably be safe," I replied. "Besides, if they do send it back, I'm sure I could do it when we get back. One more week wouldn't make that much difference."

After hiring some teenagers to feed our animals and water our garden, we were ready to go. We drove to my son's house for the first leg of the trip. We watched our granddaughter for a day while our son and his wife spent time together. Then Donna and I headed on to the coast. We found a nice hotel with an ocean view and settled in for the night. I opened my computer, and there was an email from my dissertation committee chairman.

"The next reviewer just finished. She wants the changes made by tomorrow."

I told Donna about the email.

"Have they ever told you they want it by the next day like that before?" she asked.

"Never," I replied. "They have just said to get it back as soon as possible."

We spent the next day in the hotel while I worked on the changes. Finally, in the late afternoon, I finished and returned the dissertation with the corrections.

"Well," I said with a sigh, "that should take care of it until after our vacation."

We went to a clam chowder house on the ocean and ate while we watched the sun set. We then went back to our hotel, and I opened my computer. To my dismay, there was a new email from my dissertation chairman.

"Daris, the reviewer approved the changes, and the next reviewer went through it. She would like you to make the corrections by tomorrow."

I was floored by this. They had always been at least two weeks on any review before.

I got up early the next morning and worked until we had to check out of the hotel. Donna drove to our next destination while I worked on it further. We stopped to see a few things, and in between, I continued to work. We went to a hotel earlier than we had planned, and I worked some more. Finally, exhausted, I was able to turn it in.

I complained to Donna. "Two days of our vacation had to be spent working in a hotel room. Of all the times they decided the changes had to be in by the next day, why did it have to be now?"

We enjoyed a couple of days, but the stress of it still hung over me. Then, on our last night at the coast, I opened my computer and saw another email from my committee chairman. I almost ignored it, but I finally read, "Dr. Howard, we are pleased to inform you that your dissertation has been fully and completely accepted as finalized."

I read it to my wife, and she laughed. "I guess two days of work in the hotel were worth it."

"Yeah," I said. "But now I feel like I need a vacation."

Supercharged Halloween

Although Lenny had won the last round with his uncle the previous Halloween, when he asked me if I wanted to be in on his next prank, I declined. From my record of the pranks over the years, his uncle had more wins than Lenny did. But Lenny knew he could count on Butch and Buster, and, true to form, they agreed to join him. Their success with the cat was still fresh on their minds, and they hoped to add to it.

"What do you have in mind this year?" Butch asked.

"Well," Lenny said with a sly smile, "I just happen to know that Uncle has an electric fence charger in his barn, along with some fence wire. My mom sent me to get milk from him down at his dairy barn, and I decided to scout around for an idea while he was busy milking. That's when I saw it. I hadn't ever seen it before, so I checked the old charger just to make sure it worked."

"Did you touch it?" Buster asked.

"Do I look daft to you?" Lenny said. "I put on some thick gloves and plugged in the fence charger. Then I spat on a piece of hay and touched it across the two poles of the charger. The hay lit up like a Fourth-of-July sparkler."

"Won't he miss it if we steal it?" Butch asked.

"We ain't going to steal it," Lenny said. "We're just going to borrow it for the night, and it won't even leave his property. We'll just string wire quietly around the wood fence by his house. Then, when it's all set, we'll make lots of noise. When he comes running out, he'll run right into it, and we'll get a good laugh when the jolt knocks him on his backside. The fun part will be that it's his own fencing material."

Lenny knew he couldn't nail the insulators onto the posts or his uncle would hear, so he had to figure out how he could attach them quietly. He decided he could put a wrap of electrical tape around the wire on top of the posts and then tape it down. Besides, it only had to last long enough for his uncle to touch it.

Halloween night finally came, and the three boys, dressed in black and carrying rolls of electric tape, made their way stealthily across Lenny's uncle's yard. They were almost to the barn door when Lenny, who was leading the way, slipped and fell.

"Confounded ice!" Lenny said in a loud whisper. "I don't remember there ever being ice here before."

"Must have come off the barn," Butch said.

"The barn roof slants the other way," Lenny said. "I bet my uncle put it here, hoping to stop us from pranking him."

Lenny tried to stand but slipped again. Butch and Buster tried to help, and they, too, went down.

"He can't stop us that easily," Lenny said. "Let's work together."

Holding on to each other's wrists, they formed a tripod and were able to stand. Then, still holding each other's wrists, they made their way the last few feet to the door. Lenny reached out and grabbed the doorknob. When he did, all three of them felt a charge surge through them as their hair stood on end. They all screamed, slipped, and fell. The house light came on, and the three boys started to scramble. In their hurry and confusion, they slipped and fell multiple times, often on top of each other. Eventually, they were able to crawl off the ice and run away.

At church on Sunday, the three of them were scratched and bruised. Lenny told me the story.

"Weren't you wearing gloves?" I asked. "You shouldn't have gotten shocked through gloves."

"A person can't wrap electrical tape with gloves on," Lenny said defensively.

About then, Lenny's uncle came up, smiling. "You know, my cows seem to miraculously get out on Halloween, so I decided to rig up some electric fencing." And then, as if reading our minds, he added, "They even seem to be able to open doors, so I decided I needed to electrify the doorknob to stop them."

As Lenny's uncle grinned and walked away, Lenny said, "That was not about cows at all. It was just a bunch of bull."

Wife's Time Out

When we had seven children, many of them quite young, I was working as the Internet Manager at the local university, along with teaching. My days were long and hard. When I came home, I was exhausted, but I would take time to play with my children and help around the house. But there were times when server issues kept me at work late into the night and sometimes even into the morning.

Much of the burden of taking care of the children fell to my wife, Donna, who was home most of the time. In the latter part of the fall, I could tell that she was tired, not just from lack of sleep, but from not having any time to herself. I tried to think of something that she could do that would give her a change and be something she would enjoy. One day I was looking through a brochure that came from the university, and I had a brilliant idea.

There was an Italian professor who worked in the Physics Department just down the hall from my office. The Physics Department did not have a microwave in their faculty room, but we did. So each day he would come to our department to heat up his lunch. The aroma of cheese, oregano, and many Italian herbs and spices filled the air and made my mouth water.

The paper I was looking at was the university's community classes. Anyone in the community could propose a class on a subject that they felt might be of interest to others. If the class was accepted, the person would teach the class in the evening. The class that caught my eye was one on Italian cooking to be taught by the physics teacher's wife.

My brilliant idea was that Donna could have time out for herself, and I would get to try some of the wonderful foods I smelled every day.

I took the multi-page brochure that listed the classes, and I bent the pages back so the brochure would naturally fall open to the page with the Italian cooking. I wanted to make sure it was the first thing Donna would see. I then took the brochure home and informed Donna that I was going to arrange my schedule so one night each week was hers to do something she wanted. I then handed her the brochure and suggested she find something she liked.

She excitedly thumbed through its pages. She went through it multiple times that evening. She took a few more days looking through every option. The next week, just before the classes started, she announced her choice: woodworking.

I gasped because she had never done anything like woodworking before. "Woodworking? I thought you would choose Italian cooking."

"That looks good," she replied. "But I cook much of the day every day. I want something really different."

After the shock subsided, I asked her what she would like to build.

"I was thinking about building a cupboard. I have already drawn out the plans."

She showed me her design, and I was amazed both at her skill in drawing and in her ambitious plans.

"Do you think you can finish something like this in just a couple of months with only one evening per week?" I asked.

"If not, I think I could get a long way," she replied.

The evening of the first class came, and Donna left, excited to try her hand at something new. I changed the baby, fed the children, read stories to them, and got them all in bed before Donna came home. When she did come, her hair and clothes had bits of sawdust embedded in them. She was tired and happy. And weeks later, when the last class ended, I went in to load up a beautiful cupboard, as good as any professional could make. But most important, Donna felt fulfillment in her accomplishment and new skill, and she was happy.

Maybe next fall I'll try my hand at Italian cooking.

A Real Patriot

A good friend of mine, Blaine, was a World War II veteran. He was one of the most patriotic men I knew, even if he had many reasons not to be.

As a young man, Blaine, like many others his age, found himself embroiled in the bitterness of war. After the invasion at Normandy, he was part of the army fighting across Europe toward Germany. The German army had been falling back, but as the Allied armies came closer to Berlin, the Germans dug in. The bombardment from both sides went on for days.

Blaine's unit was right at the front, and when the shelling slowed, they received the command to move forward. They ran forward toward the enemy lines, but they only got about halfway there when the Germans opened fire again.

Blaine, and all of the men with him, immediately dove for cover. They still had enough of a barrier between them and the enemy that they could defend themselves. But then something happened that was unexpected. The soldiers from the line behind them opened up with gunfire that was coming in low. Blaine saw some of his comrades fall, not from enemy fire, but from friendly fire. He also felt bullets rip into him from behind his own line.

For some time, Blaine and those with him who were still alive lay in the field as bullets whizzed around them. But eventually, for Blaine, everything went black as he passed out from loss of blood. When he woke, he was in a field hospital. They had stitched him up, but some of the bullets he had taken were impossible to remove, bullets that would cause him pain all of his life.

Blaine later found out that those who had given the order for his unit to move forward had done so without coordinating it with other levels of command. The other units could only assume he and the men with him were enemy soldiers.

Some who survived became bitter at the loss of friends and much of their own ability. Some carried that anger even to the point of bitterness against the country they served. But Blaine chose another path. He chose to let that bitter moment go from his life. He seldom shared it, but when he did, he only talked about the honor he felt being able to serve his country.

Despite his struggles, Blaine was always positive and kept a keen sense of humor. One patriotic holiday, we were standing next to each other with our hands over our hearts in honor of the flag that was being raised. There was a stiff wind, and Blaine was struggling to stay on his feet. When the halyards were securely fastened, and the flag whipped in the wind at the top of the pole, we dropped our hands.

Blaine turned to me and laughed. "I tell you, I think my hair is even more patriotic than I am. In this wind, it stands up, salutes, and stays that way for hours."

I looked to see his white hair standing straight up, and I smiled.

As Blaine was getting older and knew his days were numbered, he had one desire. He wanted to go back to Washington, D.C. to the World War II memorial to honor his friends who had never come home. But he didn't have a lot of money, and he felt that opportunity was out of his reach. Then Blaine's nephew heard of the Honor Flight, where a nonprofit group raised funds to help veterans make the trip to the war memorial honoring those with whom they served. Together Blaine and his nephew worked to fill out the necessary applications.

It seemed like forever to Blaine before he received word that he had been accepted. But when the acceptance came, he was overjoyed and shared some of his excitement with me. But sadly, Blaine never lived long enough to make the flight.

When I got a chance to go to Washington, D.C. on a business trip, I had little time for sightseeing, but I did take time on Blaine's behalf to go to the World War II memorial. As I quietly stood there with the sun setting behind me, I could almost see Blaine standing and saluting as his friends welcomed home a brother in a grand veterans' reunion. I smiled and saluted back.

Good job, my friend.

A Motivational Class

When I started college, I was a computer science major. Back then, computers were much different from what they are today. There were no computer screens as we have today. We worked on punch cards, and the punch card machines looked like big typewriters. We submitted our programs to the system administrators. They would run them through, and our output would come back on printed pages. This all took a lot of time.

Another challenge was that there were only two punch-card machines on campus that were available to students. We spent a lot of time standing in lines. It was in these lines that I did most of my homework in the first few years of my college career.

If a person was slow at typing, the line backed up a lot. Unfortunately, few people took typing in those days unless they were in office management degrees. But being in computer science, I decided that it was a skill I needed to master.

The idea scared me. I had attempted to learn piano at my mother's insistence, but I never became good at it. I was impatient, and getting my fingers and my brain to work together seemed like a Herculean task. I soon gave up. I thought that typing would be the same way, and I feared that I would fail. But I knew that if I were to become a programmer, I needed to type faster.

I signed up for the class and diligently did the assignments. When the first test came back, I was disappointed in my grade. I could tell by the groans around the room that I was not the only one.

After the teacher had finished passing out the tests, she turned to us. "You all did very poorly on this test. What is your motivation for taking this course?"

I raised my hand, and when the teacher called on me, I mentioned that I was a computer science major and needed to learn to type.

"No," the teacher said. "Deeper than that. Why are you here at college, and why are you taking any course on this campus?"

We had an in-depth discussion about the reasons, and when we boiled it all down to its core, we came to the conclusion that the reason we took any class was because of money. The whole purpose of getting an education was to be able to get a better job and thus make a better living.

"I don't want you to think of this course as typing anymore," the teacher said. "I want you to think of it for the real purpose for which you are here, and that is to make more money."

Then she did something I will never forget. "Every one of you hold your typing book to your chest," she said. Once we had done that, she said, "Now pat your books and repeat after me. Money! Money! Money!"

We followed her direction, and we all felt a little silly. Most of the class laughed. But each day after that, we started the class in the same way. We held our books to our chests, and, patting them, said, "Money! Money! Money!"

The motivation must have worked. I not only typed my papers, but I started typing papers for friends, my soon-to-be wife, and others. By the end of the semester, I obtained a speed of 145 words per minute, with around 98% accuracy. My fellow students also did much better, and the teacher was pleased with the results. But for me, the greatest takeaway from the class was a deep sense of accomplishment.

Now, as my math students struggle with their assignments, I am tempted to have them hold their books to their chests, pat them, and say, "Money! Money! Money!"

Nah. They'd probably think it was weird.

The Therapy Session

Some of us were visiting after church, and since Thanksgiving had just passed, the topic of conversation turned to turkeys. Our neighbor had one that had become rather mean. He was telling about it and how he would never raise a turkey again.

"I've raised some turkeys," I said, "and they can be as mean as any animal there is, except maybe a rooster. Turkeys and roosters think they are the cock of the walk."

Our young fourteen-year-old neighbor, McKenzie, said, "We had a really mean rooster, too. But then he had a therapy session, and everything changed."

"A therapy session?" I asked. I knew both of her parents had degrees in psychology, but that didn't sound like a fourteen-year-old.

She nodded. "It all started when our turkey was young. We put him in the chicken building because he was smaller than the hens, and we didn't think he would bother them. But because of his size, all the chickens, and especially the rooster, picked on him. We were afraid they would kill him, so we ended up having to move him to a pen of his own.

"Meanwhile, while the turkey grew up, the rooster got meaner. Every time we would try to gather eggs, the rooster would attack us. We, kids, like to gather eggs, but we were all afraid of him. That's why my dad decided that the rooster could no longer be in the henhouse.

"So we caught the rooster, and having nowhere else to put him, we put him in with the turkey. They seemed to remember each other. The rooster immediately went on the attack, and the turkey backed away as he always had. But after a few minutes, something changed. It was as if the turkey realized his old nemesis was no longer that intimidating. That was when the turkey attacked back.

"The two of them went at each other, and feathers started to fly, mostly those of the rooster. The fight was getting so bad that we eventually had to shut the door to the shed and just let them work out their differences. Mom called us to dinner, so we left the rooster and turkey to themselves. When dinner was over, we came out of the house, and everything was quiet.

"We approached the door of the building that had the rooster and the turkey in it and listened, but there was no sound. We were afraid the turkey had killed the rooster because we doubted it would be the other way around. We carefully opened the door, and the rooster, who had lodged himself up at the top of the door, fell out in a pile in the snow.

"We thought he was dead until he slowly raised his head and looked at us before dropping his head back into the snow. No one wanted to get near him in case it was an act, and he would attack, so we went back into the house for a while. But when we came back out, he was still lying there. Finally, we picked him up and put him back in the hen house for the night until we could figure out what to do with him.

"But the next day, when we went to gather eggs, the rooster didn't bother us at all. In fact, he acted all friendly-like. He has never bothered anyone since then. He's probably afraid that if he does, he will have to go through another therapy session with the turkey."

I smiled. There is nothing like a good turkey therapy session to make a mean rooster nice.

A First Name Basis

With ten children, it seemed like somebody always forgot something. Sometimes I would take time out from my day to run get the needed item. But often, what one of our children was missing was something that was left at home. Donna, my wife, often had to take the forgotten item to whichever school the child attended.

Most of the time, the child who needed something was at the middle school. Middle school is the time in life when children have gone from having everything in the classroom to being responsible for the items themselves. This change in life seems to be more of a challenge for the parents than for the child.

One day, Donna had taken an item in and was standing in the middle school office waiting to visit with the secretary. The secretary was on the phone.

"It looks like Jimmy doesn't have P.E. until fourth period, so you have time to bring his gym clothes in before class," the secretary said into the receiver.

As Donna stood waiting while the secretary continued her phone conversation, another lady came in. The lady looked flustered and embarrassed as she took her place in line behind Donna.

Donna, always sociable, turned to the lady. "Do you have to bring things in for your children often?"

"How did you know I was bringing something for my child?" the lady asked in surprise.

"That's pretty much the main reason parents come here," Donna replied. "Besides, you have a fifth-grade math book in your hand."

The lady blushed. "I guess that was kind of obvious, wasn't it?"

"Are you new here?" Donna asked. "I haven't seen you before."

The lady nodded. "Yes, we just moved here a couple months ago."

Donna held out her hand. "I'm Donna."

"It's nice to meet you," the lady said. "I'm Joan."

"I have a child in fifth-grade and one in seventh," Donna said.

"My oldest is in fifth-grade," Joan said. "And I think I have been here almost every day for the last two months. It seems there is always something. He got a power drink spilled on him and needed new clothes. He had a pop explode in his pack and needed another pack. He tore his pants and needed a replacement. He left his P.E. clothes home and would have a grade cut if he didn't have them. It just never ends. And he always calls me when I am in a hurry."

"That's the life of a parent of a middle schooler," Donna said.

"But I am afraid they will think I am annoying," Joan said.

Donna shrugged. "I'm sure we aren't the only ones. I would bet that the secretaries are used to it."

"I fear that soon the secretary and I will be on a first-name basis. I told Ross if that happens, he's going to be grounded for life."

About then, the secretary finished her phone call. She walked over to the counter.

"Donna, were you first?" the secretary asked.

Hearing her name from the secretary, Donna looked at Joan and smiled. She turned back to the secretary. "I was, Susan." Then Donna motioned toward Joan. "But I think she is in more of a hurry."

The secretary turned to Joan. "Joan, did you bring something for Ross?"

Donna grinned at the look on Joan's face when she heard her first name, along with the name of her son. After Joan handed over the math book, Donna touched her arm. "Don't ground him for too long. It's just part of his growing up."

Joan smiled. "And maybe learning patience is part of mine."

Just Need a Hug

I don't get much chance to play Santa, but I like to when I can. And I never do it for pay because that takes away from the reason I do it. Each time I get the chance to brighten the lives of children, I always feel it is I who come away better for the experience.

This year, I was Santa for a big group of children. The director sent me instructions on when to come in. At the right time, I jingled the bells in my hand and made my way into the hall. As I stood waving before going to take my place, a young girl, about three years old, came over and hugged my knees.

I knelt down and talked to her. I asked her if she was going to come up and visit with me. In wide-eyed wonder, she nodded. As she and I talked, a little boy in the first row saw me. He put down what he was playing with and came running with arms spread wide. He threw his arms around my neck and hugged me for quite some time before his mother called to him. When he pulled away, I also asked him if he was going to come up and see me. He nodded vigorously.

Once I was settled in the chair that was prepared for me, the children flocked to get in line. With the children in the group and all of their siblings, there were probably more than fifty of them.

One of the first to come to me was a little girl who was around seven. She stopped in front of me and looked right into my eyes.

"Are you the real Santa?" she asked.

I love to help children believe in the magic of Christmas, and I laughed a deep Santa chuckle. "Of course I am."

"Then am I naughty or nice?" she asked in a somewhat defiant tone.

I considered the type of child that would ask such a question and used that logic to answer. "You," I replied, "are a bit mischievous. But you are still a good girl."

I must have nailed it. Her face showed her amazement. "You *are* the real Santa!"

She then leaned up close and told me that for Christmas, she really wanted an American Girl doll. I talked to her briefly about American Girl movies, and she left with a candy cane.

One little girl asked me for a robot cat.

"Do you have a dog to terrorize with it?" She said no, so I said, "Then what fun is a robot cat?"

Her parents laughed. I told them that when I was in New York, there was a place that trained cats to be like watchdogs. They called them attack cats. But the problem was, the cats could not quickly distinguish their owners, and the cats often attacked their owners.

Near the end of the line came the boy who had hugged me. When it was his turn, I pulled him onto my lap.

"What would you like for Christmas?" I asked.

Though he was plenty old to speak, he said nothing. Instead, he threw his arms around my neck and hugged me tightly for some time. I hugged him back and felt there was more to his hug than just a child's love for the magic of Christmas. When he finally let go, and I looked into his face, he was smiling a happy smile.

"Is there anything else you want?" I asked.

He shook his head, so I grabbed a pretty blue candy cane. "I'm sure you could use this."

He gave me another big hug, smiled, took the candy cane, and headed on his way.

His mother said, "I'm sorry he hugged you so tightly and for so long."

I smiled. "It's okay. Even Santa needs hugs now and then."

"He lost his father some time ago," she said, "and he hasn't spoken a word since then. He also has hardly let anyone touch him. Maybe in Santa he feels a little of the love of his father."

After she left, I pondered what she said. Maybe there was a bigger reason I enjoyed playing the part of Santa. At this time of year, when we celebrate the birth of He who loved children most, perhaps playing Santa helps me experience a portion of that love He has for them.

The Wheelchair

Jack had loved cars since he was young. Now that he was retired, he especially loved the cars from his youth—vintage or antique cars, they were now called.

The biggest and best antique car rally was coming up, and the minute the tickets became available, Jack purchased one. He could hardly wait for the big day. His ticket was going to be his Christmas present to himself. But just before the car show, he slipped and fell, putting him in a wheelchair.

Jack was not about to let that stop him. He had a son who lived in the town where the rally was being held. Jack was sure his son would be willing to take him to the show. He called to find out.

"David, if I can get down to your place, could you get me to the car rally?" Jack asked.

"Sure, Dad," David replied. "I'd love to go to it with you, but I have to work that day."

"That's okay," Jack replied. "If you can just get me there, I can spend the day, and then you can pick me up after work."

They worked out all the details. Jack would take the bus down to the town where David lived, arriving the night before the rally. Jack would stay at David's house, and David would take him to the car rally on his way to work.

Jack checked with the bus line, and they were willing to help him on and off. They would also fold up his wheelchair and put it into the luggage storage area. He was able to get a ride to the bus from a friend and was soon settled in for the four-hour trip. David was waiting at the bus stop when Jack arrived. David's wife had a nice meal for them, then Jack retired early. He wanted to be alert for the next day and not miss a second of it.

The next morning, after a robust breakfast, Jack was ready to go to the rally. David helped Jack into his car, and they were off.

When they got to the rally, the doors were not yet open, and there was already a line. David helped Jack out of the car and into the wheelchair.

Jack knew David was supposed to be at work by eight. "David, you go to work. I'll be fine."

"Don't you want me to help you at least get into the rally?"

Jack shook his head. "I'm in line. I've got my ticket. What could go wrong?"

With one last assurance, David went to work. He worked all day and then came back to get his father. But Jack wasn't at the exhibit hall. Instead, David found out Jack was across the street at the nursing home. As David helped Jack into his car, he asked how the day went.

"What I want to know is who the idiot is who decided to build a nursing home next to an exhibit hall!" Jack said.

"Why?" David asked.

"When I got to the door and was going to show them my ticket, I couldn't find it. While I searched for it, someone decided I must have escaped from the nursing home. They wheeled me all the way there before I was able to find my ticket. They still checked with the nursing home manager to make sure I hadn't escaped before they took me back."

"But you got back and went to the show all right, didn't you?" David asked.

"Yes, but there were more than a dozen times during the day that someone thought I escaped. Sometimes they called the nursing home, and a staff member came, and sometimes the person thought they would be helpful and take me back themselves. I swear I spent half of my day trying to straighten things out so I could stay in the exhibit."

"Is that why you were at the nursing home when I picked you up?" David asked.

"Not totally," Jack said. "There was one car I really wanted to ride in, so I may have let on to the owner that I'd escaped from the nursing home, hoping he would feel sorry for me and give me a ride back. Even though it was just across the street, I figured he'd lengthen the ride around town, and I was right."

"You let the car owner think you had come from the nursing home so he'd give you a ride?" David asked in surprise. "Isn't that sneaky?"

"All I can say," Jack replied, "is if a man is dealt a bad hand, he should use it to his advantage."

A Shocking Discovery
(Part 1)

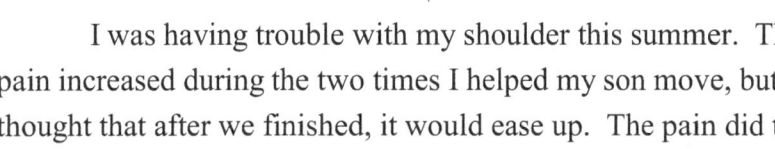

I was having trouble with my shoulder this summer. The pain increased during the two times I helped my son move, but I thought that after we finished, it would ease up. The pain did taper off, but it was still almost unbearable. I finally decided I had to have it checked.

The doctor moved my arm through a lot of different rotations. He said he was sure there were torn ligaments. He wanted me to get an MRI to make sure, so I set an early morning appointment with the imaging lab so I could get it over with and get on with my day.

On the appointed morning, I arrived at eight and filled out the paperwork. It wasn't long after I turned it in that I was called back.

"Do you have any problems with claustrophobia?" the technician asked.

"Some," I replied. "But I think if I just keep my eyes closed, I will be okay."

"This will only take about eighteen minutes," he said. "You will have headphones on, partly because the machine is loud and partly so we can play music. Music usually helps calm a person."

The technician examined my shoulder. "Do you have any metal in your arm?"

I shook my head. "No. Why do you ask?"

"You have some interesting scarring on your shoulder. If you were to have any metal in it, the metal could heat up in the machine."

I climbed onto the table. The technician wrapped a cap-shaped item around my shoulder and handed me a remote with a button on it. He told me to press it if there was any problem.

I laid back and closed my eyes, and the bed moved me into the machine. He turned on the music, and the sound and vibration started. But it had been on less than a minute when it all shut down.

He came on over the headphones. "You have a bullet in your arm."

"How can I have a bullet in my arm and not know it?" I asked.

He laughed. "Shouldn't I be the one asking *you* that question?"

He hit the buttons to have the bed move me back out, and he talked to me.

"Were you in the military and possibly picked up some shrapnel?" When I told him I wasn't, he said, "I suppose it could be picking up something on your shirt."

He had me take my shirt off and roll the sleeve on my undershirt up beyond my shoulder. He again put the cap piece over my arm, and I climbed back on the table. Once I was back in place, he started the machine up again. Once more, the MRI machine was on less than a minute before he shut it down. He spoke over the speaker.

"There is definitely a bullet in your shoulder. It will probably get warm and maybe even really hot. I can try to work around it and still do the MRI, but it has to be your choice."

"Let's do it," I said.

"All right, but if it starts to get too hot, hit the button."

He started the machine up again, and the spot he indicated had the bullet did get hot, but not unbearably so. It also felt like tiny pins were poking me all around that spot. By the time the test was done, that part of my shoulder was tingling enough to nearly drive me crazy.

After I put my shirt back on, I asked if he would show me the bullet on the MRI.

He brought up the image, and I asked, "Do you think that's what is causing my problem?"

"I'm a technician, not a doctor," he said. "I'm not allowed to even guess. But I do have a question. Surely you have some idea where it came from, don't you?"

"Oh, I have some ideas," I replied, "but the strange thing is there are too many possibilities to be sure."

When I walked out of there, all I could think about was how strange it was to be told you have a bullet in your arm and not know for sure where it came from.

A Bullet in My Arm
(A Shocking Discovery part 2)

After I got over the shock of seeing the bullet in my arm on the MRI, curiosity started to get the best of me. I thought of the years of my life and when it possibly could have happened. I also realized that the bullet was probably why every time I had gone through airport screening, I was pulled aside by the security personnel so they could use their magic wand along my leg and my arm. My leg was understandable. It was held together with more bolts than a car chassis. But now, for the first time, I understood why they had wanded my arm. Still, the question lingered as to where the bullet came from.

When I went to work, my colleagues asked what the MRI had shown. When I mentioned the bullet, they were almost as shocked as I was. When they found out I didn't even know exactly where or when I had gotten it, they were even more surprised.

"You can't go around telling people you were shot and don't even remember it," one of them said. "You need to make up a good story to go with it."

"Like what?" I asked.

"I think you should tell people you were abducted by aliens," he replied.

"And they shot me? Why would aliens shoot me?"

He shrugged. "Tell people you were escaping, and they were firing at you."

When my one son heard about the bullet, he laughed. "At work, some of the other men sit around and tell tough-man stories. Wait until I tell them that my father is so tough that he got shot and didn't even know it."

Pretty much everyone who heard the story had some sarcastic comment. But, if possible, I still hoped to find out where and when I got it. So I turned to the one person I thought might have an answer. I called my mother.

"Mom, do you have any idea where or when I could have gotten a bullet in my arm?" I asked.

She gasped. "What are you talking about?"

I told her the story and then asked, "So, do you remember anything that might give me a clue?"

My mom let out a disgusted sigh. "Absolutely not! But knowing you and your friends when you were younger, it doesn't surprise me one bit. It's a wonder you ever survived to adulthood."

I had to smile at that. Butch and Buster were interesting. They had grown up hunting, even as small boys, and they shot guns a lot. They not only used guns for hunting and for target practice; they sometimes shot at each other. That one is definitely a story for another day, but I started to consider that it was likely during one of those times with them that I had picked up a stray bullet. It was probably from a ricochet from something we were shooting at.

My mom is living with my sister, so my sister got on the phone to talk to me. "But Daris, how, if you got shot when you were with your friends, did you not notice it? Surely you were bleeding."

"Oh, I'm sure I must have been bleeding," I replied. "But we often came in covered with mud and bleeding from our adventures. I probably just thought it was something else and didn't pay too much attention to it."

One of my neighbors worked with Buster. Out of curiosity, to see what Buster would say, my neighbor casually mentioned the bullet and the fact that I wasn't sure where it came from.

"Oh, my heck," Buster said. "Me or my brother probably accidentally shot him."

When I heard about his reaction, I laughed and remembered a day when it might have happened.

A Possible Answer

(A Shocking Discovery - part 3)

Having found out during an MRI that I had a bullet in my arm, I thought back upon a possible answer as to when it could have happened.

One day, my friend Buster invited me over after school. He wanted to show me his pigeons. "After all," he said, "you helped me capture them from your barn."

He loved his pigeons. We had gotten them as babies, and he had raised them and trained them. But when we got to his house, we found the pigeon coop had been destroyed.

Buster lived with his father, two brothers, a sister, and Granny. They had moved here from the mountains of West Virginia. Buster was the oldest of the children, with Butch only a year younger. I was friends with both of them, but they were always at odds with each other.

Buster angrily looked at the destroyed pigeon coop. "I betcha Butch did it," he said.

It wasn't until later that we learned that Buster's dad had destroyed the coop, feeling the pigeons were a source of contention in the family. But if the pigeons had been a source of contention in the past, they were about to be more so now. Buster grabbed an ax and headed to the garage.

"What are you doing?" I asked.

He didn't even slow his pace as he answered. "I'm gonna to teach Butch not to mess with me!"

Butch had an expensive skateboard he loved. Buster got it and put it on the chopping block. I knew what he had in mind and tried to talk him out of it, but he wouldn't be deterred. Soon the skateboard was nothing but a bunch of plastic splinters. Having accomplished his design, Buster put the ax away, and we went to his bedroom.

Buster was lying on his bed, and I was sitting on a chair as we talked. Suddenly, Butch kicked the door into pieces, busting his way into the room. He jumped on Buster and started to pound him. Buster reached over onto a nightstand, grabbed a solid bronze statue, and smacked Butch over the head with it, knocking him unconscious.

"Oh, my heavens!" Buster said, as Butch rolled to the floor, "I've killed him!" Buster ran to his closet and started stuffing clothes into a duffle bag. "I'm heading to Mexico. I'll let you know when I get there."

Before Buster could become a fugitive, Butch started to revive. After he did, it was all-out war. We were about twelve years old, that ripe old age when about half the decisions we made were wrong, and the other half were stupid. Butch and Buster's dad had decided that they were old enough to be responsible, so he had given each of them a .22 rifle for Christmas. I seriously don't know what he was thinking.

They for their guns, and I headed out of the house. But, of course, so did they. It wasn't long before we were all three in the backyard. Each of them was hunkered down behind a log or boulder. One would pop up and fire off some shots at the other. He would then drop down, and the other one would sit up and fire off some rounds in response.

As for me, I stayed down and listened to the bullets whizzing around me. I thought to myself, "This would probably be a good time to go home." But staying down and living to tell the story was the preferable option at the moment.

Eventually, Granny appeared at the back door. She quickly figured out what was going on.

"Butch, Buster, you put those guns away before I come out there and beat you with them! Do you hear me? You bring those guns to me, and I mean now! If either of you fires one more shot, you is gonna wish you was dead!"

Butch and Buster knew better than to defy Granny. She had worked most of her life in the coal mines alongside the men. Butch and Buster sheepishly came out of their hiding places and brought Granny their guns. I used that time to start walking the three miles home, heading for the safety of my boring chores.

As I thought back about that experience, I realized that might have been when I got the bullet in my arm. But then, maybe not. There were so many like it; maybe it was one of the others.

Shoulder Surgery

(A Shocking Discovery - Part 4)

After finding out there was a bullet in my arm, I hoped that was what was causing the pain in my arm. I figured that if a bullet was removed, there would be less trauma and healing than if it was torn ligaments. But I was to have no such luck. The doctor told me there was indeed a bullet in my arm, like the MRI technician had said, but it wasn't causing me any problems. The real problem was that I needed a rotator cuff repair.

We looked at available surgery dates. I wanted to get it done before Christmas so I would have more time to heal before going back to work in January. But I needed to move the harp for my daughter until December 22nd. That only left December 24th for the surgery date. I had the nurse schedule it. Later, when I met with my family, I let them know.

"Can we have Christmas on the 23rd?" my daughter asked. "If we have it on Christmas right after you have had your surgery, you will probably be grouchy. I'd rather not have my father be grouchy on Christmas."

I told her I didn't think I would be grouchy, but agreed to celebrate Christmas on the 23rd anyway. It ended up being a nice day. We opened presents and then invited another daughter that lived close by to bring her family and join us when we went out to eat. We scheduled it so her husband could come from work during his lunch hour. It was fun.

The next day, as I headed to the hospital, I must admit that all I could think about was when I was 45 I got my tonsils removed. For two hours before being wheeled back, I was in a room where the broken tv could not be shut off and was locked onto a channel that played only Barney reruns. By the time they came to get me, I was feeling like, "Just shoot me now!"

However, this time the room I was put in for surgery preparation didn't even have a tv. I was okay with that. Many people came in to take my vitals and talk to me about recovery. Four of them asked me which shoulder was being operated on. When I told them it was my left, they marked it with a marker.

As the fourth person made his mark, I said, "Don't you trust the other three people who marked it already?"

He laughed. "A person can never be too careful."

After he left, I told my wife, Donna, to hand me a marker.

"Why?" she asked.

"I think I ought to put marks all over me just to confuse them."

She did not think that was even funny and made sure there were no markers anywhere in the room. She said that removing my access to markers was her part of being careful.

Eventually, I was wheeled into the surgery room.

The anesthesiologist leaned over me. "It will take about ten minutes for you to fade off to sleep."

Ten minutes, nothing. I was out almost instantly after he said it, and if I said anything past that point, I want to make it clear that I can't legally be held responsible for it. The next thing I remember was having someone patting me, calling me by name, and asking me how I was doing.

"Did you get the number?" I groggily replied.

"Of what?" she asked.

"Of the license plate of the truck that hit me."

I heard my wife laugh. "I think he's going to be fine."

And I'm not admitting that I was grouchy. But my daughter was probably smart to have had us celebrate Christmas on the 23rd.

And the bullet? Well, it remains in my arm as a souvenir of some exciting day from my youth. I just wish I could remember which day.

I Can Do My Own Yard, Thank You

It seemed the minute I had shoulder surgery and had my arm in a sling, the snow started coming and never let up. We didn't worry too much about it during Christmas break, but in the first part of January, after work and school started again, the snow needed to be shoveled.

A lot of the burden fell on my wife, Donna, but I learned how to shovel snow with one arm. I would grab the shovel below the handle and wrap the handle under my forearm. I found I could shovel snow quite efficiently, though I did have to do smaller scoops.

However, it seemed like we would just finish shoveling from one snowstorm only to have another one hit. I was trying to help all I could, and Donna was concerned that I was not being careful enough with the arm I had surgery on. It was during one of these snow shoveling sessions that she suggested we should get a four-wheeler to push the snow.

"We aren't getting any younger," she said. "And this issue is just going to come back year after year and be more vexing to us."

"Our neighbors have been kind to help us out while my arm heals," I replied. "And a four-wheeler is a lot of money."

She nodded. "I understand all of that. But these types of health challenges are going to happen more and more. I know how independent you are, and you definitely don't want to have to rely on someone to always do it for us."

I had to agree with her, so we started looking for a four-wheeler. We had never purchased one before, so we talked to all of our neighbors and friends who owned one. They helped us know what to look for in our search. Finally, we narrowed it down to a few, and after some test runs, we bought one.

We had no sooner got it home than my wife and daughters were vying for who got to clean the driveway. I, unfortunately, was not even in the running. I can't run the machine with one hand. I didn't even get to try it out before we bought it.

It wasn't long before our driveway was scraped clean, with the snow pushed into big piles at the side. Areas we don't usually use in the winter were even scraped clean. When Donna came in, I complimented her.

"It really looks good. You are really getting the hang of running that machine."

She let out a disgusted sigh. "Yeah, well, the neighbors did half of it before I even had a chance." She paused a moment, and her eyes lit up. "I wonder if there are any neighbors that need me to clear their driveways."

We talked about it further and came to the agreement that she should get some more practice before she did it for someone else.

"But that's the problem," she said. "If someone keeps clearing our driveway before I can, how am I supposed to get any practice?"

Sunday came, and quite a few people had heard about our new machine and were happy for us. One lady told us she had just sold her four-wheeler. Before Donna could offer to come to help clean her yard, the lady continued.

"In its place, my husband bought me a little tractor with a scraper and a loader."

"How do you like it?" I asked.

"How should I know?" she replied. "I haven't got to use it all winter. Before I can, some neighbor comes and scrapes my driveway. I'm dying to try out my tractor, but there is nothing left to try it on after the neighbors finish. I want to run out there and say, 'I can do my own yard, thank you,' but they have it done before I even get a chance to tell them. I keep wondering if there is anyone who needs to have their yard cleaned so I can try out my tractor."

I looked at Donna and smiled. She gave me a look that told me not to even say what I was thinking. But we both knew she probably wasn't going to get any extra practice with our new four-wheeler.

What Students Learned in Math Class 2020

Over the years, I have found that one of the students' greatest criticisms of any math class is their claim that they didn't learn anything. Therefore, as part of their final, I have the students list ten things that they have learned. These items can be anything at all in relation to the class. They are allowed to write their list ahead of time and bring it to the final if they want. Most observations are quite normal, but some make for interesting reading. It has been a while since I have shared any, so I thought I'd do so here.

1) I learned that your best odds in gambling come from not doing it at all.

2) I learned that math is easier the second time around and can even be understood the second time.

3) I learned that skipping class is hard on your grade.

4) I learned that Jessica, the girl sitting next to me, works at Victoria's Secret and can get great discounts. *(Written by a girl)*

5) I learned that Professor Howard was right. Sitting closer to the front reduces distraction and helps me learn better.

6) I learned that I should have paid more attention in high school.

7) I learned I should have went [sic] to the writing center sooner to learn how to write better.

8) I learned that the guy next to me overreacts about everything.

9) I learned that math is used in almost everything. This really stinks for those of us who are mathematically impaired.

10) One of the things I learned that will stick with me the most is your quote "If you are not failing now and then, you are not reaching high enough." I was always afraid of failure, but now I realize it is a normal part of becoming better.

11) I learned that college isn't like what I did in high school. It is important to listen the first week so you know there are assignments due right from the beginning.

12) I learned I am more than happy to pay an accountant to do my taxes rather than do them myself. They are confusing.

13) I learned that when I feel good about a test, I probably did bad. But I also learned that if I feel bad about a test, I still did bad.

14) I learned that it is fun when the teacher makes a small mistake on the board, and no one catches it until he has worked the problem for 15 minutes. It is fun watching him have to redo all of it once he gets to the end and realizes something is wrong. Of course, my problem is I get to the end and don't realize something is wrong even when it is.

15) I learned the only way to really do well in math is to do the homework until it is understood, not just finished.

16) The most annoying thing ever is when someone brings food that has a strong smell into class, especially if it doesn't smell very good. Of course, since I have been morning sick, nothing smells good.

17) I have built a good relationship with my calculator, and we have become friends. I didn't like it very much before.

18) I learned not to come late the second day of class when we mark our seat on the seating chart, or I get stuck at the front by the projector screen.

19) I learned that if I plan to be an artist or a freelance writer, I better marry a man that makes a good living. When we did our budget project, I found out I would be in a lot of trouble because I probably wouldn't make much.

20) I learned that Cassie, the girl sitting next to me, is very obnoxious and funny, while Professor Howard is very kind and funny.

21) I learned that my girlfriend is in love with my roommate.

22) I learned that Professor Howard is highly entertaining, spiritually motivated, and numerically inclined, while still wearing 70's style clothes.

Walk in Someone Else's Shoes

The recent corona virus outbreak, and the fear surrounding it, remind me of a story I heard. It was based on an event during the 1918 Spanish Flu epidemic.

Earl was a hard-working, family-oriented man. He, his wife, and their children ran a little country store in a small western town. In the area where they lived, there was a lot of excitement about a new branch of the railroad that would be coming through.

When the rail line work started, many new people came. Most of these were families of men who were working on the railroad. Earl's business increased significantly. But bringing the goods in was costly. Everything had to come over the mountain on mules and wagons until the rail line was finished, .

Earl tried to keep his prices fair. He only added enough markup on goods to pay his costs and take care of his family. But many people complained about the prices at Earl's store. Most of these were people who had come from other towns much farther south. These towns already had train service and didn't have the added transportation costs.

Earl and his family had endured the anger and name-calling for some time when the flu epidemic hit. Of all the families in the town, his family was hit the hardest. Many people came in and out of his store, and many carried the flu. Soon, Earl's whole family was sick.

Though Earl worked from morning until night taking care of his family, he tried to keep his store open as much as possible. He knew the people of the town depended on it. But Earl lost four of his six children, and his wife was bedridden. There were days he had to shut the store to bury his children or just take care of his family. This added more to the anger he received from those who came to town only to find the store closed.

One day, when Earl was driving to the cemetery with the body of his two-year-old daughter in a small pine box, a crowd surrounded his wagon. They started yelling things at him about being rich while others struggled, and him not caring about anyone else. Suddenly, the crowd went crazy. Someone pulled Earl from the wagon, and men began beating him.

Almost instantly, the railroad foreman was there. He knew of the losses Earl had in his family and had even helped Earl bury some of his children. The foreman angrily hit and kicked his way into the circle, single-handedly forcing the men to stop. The foreman helped Earl to his feet, then climbed onto the wagon and held up the small coffin as he spoke.

"You bunch of fools! You blame Earl for your problems when you don't even know what real problems are. In this box lies the body of his youngest daughter, the fourth of his children he has had to bury. Which one of you would be willing to trade him places? Which of you would be willing to take his store in exchange for those you love?"

The foreman then turned to one of the men who was foremost in the beating. "How about you, John? You haven't lost a single family member to the flu. Which one of your children's lives would you like to trade for Earl's store? How about Timothy or maybe little Susan?"

John couldn't even look at the foreman as he shook his head. The foreman asked a similar question of others and received a similar response.

"Well, then," the foreman said, "when you imagine how much better you think it is for someone else, I'd suggest you consider what it would be like to walk in their shoes all the way, not just on the parts of their journey that you like."

The foreman reached out a hand and pulled Earl back onto the wagon. He then turned to the crowd. "I suggest you get back to your work. As for me, I plan to go to the cemetery and help dig a small grave."

As Earl and the foreman drove to the cemetery, no one returned to their work. Instead, they followed the wagon. As many men helped dig the small grave next to the three new markers that were already there, no one said a word. But as Earl fell to his knees sobbing when the little wooden box was placed into its place, people in that small country town were changed forever.

As years passed, people who came to that town said there was never a town with more compassion. The old-timers would nod and say it was because those who lived there had to learn the hard way what it was like to walk in someone else's shoes.

A Desire to Help

It was 1918, and Arden, the man Rachel had been dating, was off fighting in the Great War. Rachel worked hard on the farm and in her grandfather's store as a clerk, but there were times she felt like she wasn't doing enough to help. Then she started seeing those around her falling ill to what had been dubbed the Spanish flu and felt she just had to do something.

Some families lost more than half of their family members, while some families were so ill, they couldn't take care of each other. Rachel approached her parents about her concerns.

"You know you could catch the flu, and it might take your life?" her father said.

Rachel nodded. "But if I live unscathed, and didn't do what I could to help, I doubt I could live with myself."

Her parents understood her feelings, and they agreed to help. Rachel's family started organizing food boxes to go to families who were quarantined in their homes. Rachel and her brothers would deliver them. But Rachel felt still she had to do more. There was so much suffering. One small town lost almost fifty percent of the people in it to the flu.

One day a young doctor came to Rachel's grandfather's store while she was there. He was looking for a nurse assistant to work for him. He had been all over the valley, to hospitals and medical schools, but everyone was afraid to go into the homes of those who were ill. He felt that was the only way to stop this pandemic.

"What will you do when you go into the home?" Rachel asked.

"Most of the quarantined homes are shut up tight," the doctor answered. "That just locks the flu inside with those who live there. We need to go into the homes and open up doors and windows, let in fresh air, and clean the bedding."

Rachel took a deep breath for courage and volunteered. Her family was frightened for her but supported her decision. The hard work then began.

She and the doctor would go into the homes. The first thing they would do was get everyone tucked into bed where they could be warm, then Rachel and the doctor opened the windows and doors so fresh air and sunlight could enter the house. Then Rachel worked at washing bedding and clothes and hanging them to dry in the sun while the doctor attended to the sick. Within a few days, some of the family would begin to recover and could take over, then Rachel and the doctor would move to the next family.

Rachel's family would bring supplies to help, but Rachel made them leave the supplies outside and keep their distance. She was afraid of infecting them if she was carrying the flu. The months went on, and the flu started to ease up. Rachel looked forward to the time it would end, and when Arden would also come home. But just as it looked like the end of the flu was in sight, the inevitable happened, and both Rachel and the young doctor became sick.

Hundreds of people owed their lives to the two of them, and there was no end of those wanting to return the favor. Following the doctor's own advice, the makeshift hospital he and Rachel were put in had windows and doors open for air and sunlight. Though their symptoms were severe, both pulled through, and not long afterward, the flu was declared to be under control.

Having done what he set out to do, the doctor now felt free to marry the young lady he had waiting. Arden came home, and it wasn't long before he and Rachel also married. And as the years passed, Rachel watched children she had loved and cared for grow to marry and have children of their own.

And seeing the exemplary lives of those who likely would not have made it if she had not been willing to help always made her own life just a little better.

Reluctance to Technology

With the coronavirus in full swing, the university where I work had shut down face-to-face classes and moved everything online. We had to teach our students from the enclosure of our offices. The previous summer, I finished a doctorate in online education with an emphasis on technology, so this situation provided an opportunity to use the training I received.

As the university decided to shut down our face-to-face classes, I quickly realized my computer camera was mediocre at best. My department committed to purchasing new equipment, including better webcams and document readers. But that ran into an immediate snag, as many other schools did the same thing. Most items were put on backorder and would not arrive until after the semester is over.

I spent hours testing for the best camera angle and lighting to illuminate my whiteboard. I created guidelines, documents, and software for my students who would need them. I sent out emails with step-by-step instructions for the students to join me for our first class together.

There were a few snags I had to iron out, but by the time I taught my first set of online classes, things went well. I made mistakes, but I had set a second computer in the background and logged it in as a student. With this computer I could see what the students saw and quickly knew if something was wrong. Some students struggled with the change, but most accepted it quite well.

While I was working through this, I thought of my mother and her reluctance to accept new technology. It was her ninety-fourth birthday just a couple of weeks ago. For Christmas two years ago, my sister gave Mom an Alexa so Mom wouldn't feel so alone in her apartment. The first time Alexa talked to Mom, she was frightened and thought there was an intruder in her apartment. It took her a while to calm down and get used to Alexa, but she finally did.

Back when Mom lived by us, she would come over for dinner, and my teenage daughter would tell Mom the newest jokes she had heard. One day Mom called, and I had the phone on speaker. When she found out that my daughter could hear her, she said, "Elli, check out this Alexa."

Mom then asked Alexa to tell her a joke. When Alexa finished, Mom laughed and laughed. But Alexa was clear across the room, so the only words I could make out from the joke were "the Beatles." I asked Mom what the joke was, and she said, "I don't know. I didn't get it."

It was just a machine talking to her that she found funny.

Last fall, I picked Mom up, and we drove four hours to a wedding. I was not familiar with the address, so when we got to the city where the wedding was, I turned on Google Maps.

Mom shook her head in disgust. "I don't know why you use that foolish thing. I'm sure I can tell you directions better than that phone lady can."

As we drove, the maps program said, "In 100 feet, turn right."

"No, no, no!" Mom said. "That's wrong. I used to come up here all the time."

"But, Mom," I said. "That was decades ago, and things change. The computer has it all programmed in."

"Well, I don't trust her," Mom said. "I'm sure she's taking us the wrong way."

About that point, Mom remembered that she had wanted to stop and get a wedding card.

"No problem," I said. "I will just have my phone tell us where the nearest drug store is."

The phone said there was one just fifty feet ahead on the left.

Mom let out a disgusted grunt. "Now you'll see how stupid your phone lady is. There's no drug store within ten miles of here."

Mom was just finishing saying that as I turned the car into the drug store's parking lot. Mom looked up and saw where we were, and as she turned and scowled at me, I didn't even dare smile.

Mom glared at me and said, "And just for your information, I still don't trust her."

A Silver Lining

Like many of you, I am affected by the shut down because of the coronavirus. I am now teaching my college students online from my living room. I miss the face-to-face interaction with them, and I worry about their safety and whether some of them will finish the semester. Some of them have only half-heartedly done their work since we had to quit meeting in the classroom.

The shutdown has also affected my family. My youngest daughter, Elliana, is our last child at home. This is her senior year, and she is missing out on end-of-year school plays, concerts, and graduation activities. We had her senior harp recital scheduled for Saturday, March 21. That was that week that the government leaders gave the shutdown orders.

We found out we couldn't use the rented hall only two days before the scheduled day. Her recital, which was supposed to be held in a room for fifty, was instead held in our living room. Besides my wife, Donna, and me, four other people came. They were Elli's sister, two neighbors who wouldn't miss it for anything, and Elli's teacher. Everyone sat six feet apart. We also broadcast it on the internet.

As with almost anything that doesn't turn out as you wish, there was a silver lining. Around 150 people tuned in online to watch Elli's performance, with another two hundred watching it when it was posted on Facebook. After I posted the videos on her website, harmonyharpist.com, more people viewed them. We had expected that maybe thirty people would come to the performance, so the online recital had higher attendance than we had imagined. And lots of people, who were sequestered in their homes, wrote about how much they enjoyed having something good to attend, even if it was only online.

There was another upside, at least for me. Elli had spent the previous days making cookies and brownies for an estimated fifty people. For a couple of weeks, I have had all the brownies and cookies I could eat, which brings me to another unexpected plus from all these challenges.

Donna taught the children to cook from the time they were young, but since Elli was graduating this year, Donna insisted Elli plan full meals. With our other children, the semester they were graduating, they were assigned to do one meal each week with their mother's help. But Elli chose instead to take a cooking class at school. She would come home and tell us all about the tasty things she had made, and I felt left out.

But now, since schools are closed, she cannot cook there anymore. But just because the students are not going to their schools does not mean the education process has ended. The teachers send out assignments that the students must do at home. And you guessed it—Elli has to cook.

Her cooking assignments are not just once per week. Each week she must make up to three different dishes. She has made some delicious meals. One night she made some incredible chicken enchiladas. Another night I came home to the tantalizing smell of Chicken Alfredo. She has made desserts and main dishes, lunches and dinners, and evening snacks. And, of course, as part of the class, she needs someone to test her creations and give feedback.

That is where I come in. I am good at tasting things. And everything Elli made was delicious. A downside is my weight has been going up. However, we started praying and fasting regularly for those who have gotten sick, and that has helped with the weight issue.

I have been watching the goodness of people helping each other and sharing what they have. I'm not good at too many things, but I have shared extra toilet paper and helped where I could. I have seen others share food, encouragement, and service of all kinds. I envision that just like most hard things, we will emerge from this trial a better, kinder, and more united people.

And that will be the greatest silver lining of all.

Stir Crazy

Parents feel the challenge of being home with their children who are going stir crazy since they can't play with others their age. But how do the children feel when they are trying to find something to do? My wife, Donna, has lots of friends on the internet, and one friend, Katie Vaughan, shared her story.

Katie is the mother of a blended family with a darling four-year-old son named Porter. Katie likes to use Amazon Prime. As a mother, it is much more convenient to order something and have it show up at her door than to run out to make the purchase.

Porter had seen his mother using Amazon and understood the connection between his mom finding something she wanted to purchase and the mailman dropping it off on their porch. Sometimes Porter would ask to look at toys on Amazon, and Katie would key the word into Amazon's search bar. For those of us who are older, we might well remember looking at Sears and Roebuck or J. C. Penney catalogs before Christmas. Amazon is today's equivalent.

One day, Porter asked his mother if he could look at dunk tanks on Amazon. Katie figured that he must have seen one on YouTube and was interested in looking at it further. Porter brought Katie her iPad, and she keyed in the search for dunk tanks. She was quite surprised to find out that Amazon did sell them. But she felt it couldn't do any harm to let her little son look at them.

A little while later, Porter brought his mother back the iPad and said the mailman would deliver them a dunk tank. Katie smiled at this. Children will often find something they want only to see Santa magically deliver it. So why should a child not think the same thing could happen with the mailman? Katie just shrugged it off. But that quickly changed when she received the email confirmation of an Amazon order for a $3500 dunk tank a few minutes later.

Katie could hardly believe her small son knew how to follow through and complete the order on her account. He was so pleased with himself that Katie couldn't be mad and instead just laughed about it. She was able to cancel the order. She knew Porter didn't understand about the money, nor did he understand about an order getting canceled. Needless to say, Katie changed her Amazon settings so it was more difficult to checkout.

Katie's story, and the strangeness we have seen with the run on toilet paper, reminded me of a similar story on the radio about six months back. On Sundays, for church, a lady listened to an internet preacher. He was lamenting the fact that so much of what we do these days is impersonal, disconnected, and online. (I found that to be interesting since he was an internet preacher.) To get his point across, he gave an example.

"We don't even go to the store anymore to buy something essential like toilet paper. Instead, we just say, 'Alexa, order me fifty giant cases of toilet paper,' and then we have it delivered to our door. We don't ever see or even talk to another person, only a machine."

You can guess what happened. A few days later, a semi-truck backed into the lady's driveway. The driver got out and said, "Lady, where do you want your fifty cases of toilet paper?"

It just happened that her Alexa was on as the preacher was preaching. It had dutifully ordered her toilet paper, as it was told to do. She was floored by this and didn't know what to do with all of it. If that had been today, she would know and could have sold it and doubled her money.

But back to the story about Katie. Trying to explain to her little son that she had canceled the order did no good. He was sure it would come and kept sneaking out each day when the mailman arrived to see if the dunk tank had been delivered.

Katie just smiled and decided that she needed to rent a dunk tank for her little son's next birthday party.

The Stay-At-Home Challenge

Sometimes it is hard to find humor in our current situation. But I got an email the other day with an ad regarding having to stay at home during the pandemic. It was about exercise equipment. It started by saying, "Let's talk about the elephant in the room—you. Yes, you. You, the elephant in the room. You know I am talking about you because you are sitting around getting fat."

Okay, so maybe it didn't really say it in those words, but it implied it. Then it went on to advertise the exercise equipment, along with videos and online groups a person could connect with to help them keep their weight down. It implied that if a person were to stay healthy and fit, they would survive the health challenges that were thrown at them a lot better.

I do believe that is true, but there is something that tosses a wrench in the works for me. Years ago, I was trying to save a calf and myself from being killed by a pack of coyotes. It was thirty to forty degrees below zero, and I had to run for my life carrying the calf. I froze my lungs so severely that I had pneumonia for weeks. It still affects me. It makes me think that if I end up getting the covidvirus, I would have about as much chance of survival as an ant in a gully during a thunderstorm.

For that reason, my thought process brings me to consider that if I am possibly going to die, why not die happy? Happy, of course, meaning dying surrounded by family and at least ten pounds of chocolate.

So, back to the advertisement. Scrolling through it, I saw page after page and image after image of people doing all sorts of exercises in tandem with others connected on screen. But I immediately knew it was a big gimmick, and there was no truth to it.

How, you might ask, was I able to see through this false advertising so quickly? It was really easy. All the people in the advertisement pictures, who were sweating and working out like

Spartans ready to go to battle, were smiling. No one smiles while they are doing agonizing muscle-burning, gut-wrenching exercises unless they are in Junior Miss trying to impress judges, or are being paid to lie on commercials.

To make matters worse, Easter came right in the middle of the stay-at-home order. Easter is that holiday where a burrowing, gregarious, plant-eating mammal with long ears, long hind legs, and a short tail (thanks, Oxford dictionary) brings truckloads of chocolate to everyone. Easter is my worst self-indulging celebration. Chocolate-covered marshmallow eggs are even better than anything the big jolly guy brings at Christmas time.

Even though my two youngest children who are currently at home include one from college and a senior in high school, we still go all-out for tradition. Unfortunately, back before the epidemic hit, I bought candy more like when we had all ten of our children at home. Back in those days, the two Easter bunnies in my house took hours to figure the right hiding places for everyone's Easter basket. The younger children got the easiest hiding places, and the older children had the hardest ones.

The Easter bunnies were always kind to my wife and me and hid our Easter baskets in plain sight. But one year, my older children snuck home early from church and hid my Easter basket in the hardest place they could find. It was days before I found it. Okay, so it wasn't days, maybe hours, or probably ten minutes. But by the time I found it, I was a chocolate-deprived Tasmanian devil after a chocolate Bugs Bunny, ready to eat all candy in my path.

So, you may ask what I have done to try to keep my weight even minutely below blimp-size on the fat register. The answer is gardening. The weather is finally warming enough that the snow pile outside our north window is down to only four feet high. The garden raking and cleaning has brought me closer to thinking about carrots, cabbage, and cucumbers instead of bunnies bearing bonbons.

The fresh air and sunshine, along with the thought of the reward of good things to eat, make it the best exercise of all.

A Sense of Community

Besides being a group of people living in the near vicinity of each other, the dictionary defines community as "a feeling of fellowship with others, as a result of sharing common attitudes, interests, and goals." This definition has taken on a different meaning over the last six months.

Here in the farming community of Idaho where I live, the harvest season has a short window. Equipment runs from before sunup to after sundown, and many people are involved. Many people who have other jobs during the rest of the year end up working on sorting crews, driving a truck, or running farm equipment. It is exhausting work.

Usually, the harvest is well underway when the first frost hits. Then the weather warms, and everything kicks into overdrive for a couple of weeks, because all the crops need to be stored before harder frosts come and destroy them.

But this year was different. Harvest was in full swing when the first frost hit, but that frost was followed by even harder frosts in quick succession night after night. Potatoes could not be harvested because the weather was too cold.

Generally, with the first frost, the potatoes in the ground are still protected by the soil. But with the continued hard frosts, the ground froze deeper and deeper, and along with it, more and more potatoes were destroyed.

When a break in the weather finally came, farmers found the top layers of potatoes were mushy and useless. Not only was the harvest seasoned now drastically shortened, but the amount of work to separate the bad potatoes from the good had exponentially increased the labor needed to harvest the potatoes that could be saved.

The wonderful people of this valley, seeing the plight of their neighbors whose livelihoods depended on that harvest, came together, most as volunteers for no pay, to help get those crops in. There were people from all walks of life—bankers, merchants, and teachers—lots of good neighbors and friends. Though some of the harvest was lost, much of it was saved.

Now, with the pandemic, I have seen that sense of community again, but on an even wider scale. Social media groups have been formed where people can ask for help. In many of them, there are more people asking how they can help than there are asking for help.

It was heartwarming when I saw a mother, who had sick children and needed to stay home with them, ask for someone to pick up cough medicine for her child. The response was almost immediate, with multiple offers of help. Soon the desperate mother had what she needed, but only after the caring person had gone to numerous stores to find one that had the medicine in stock.

Though I have read about places that are price gouging, I have seen the opposite. Neighbors have shared food, toilet paper, and other essential items without any thought of being repaid. And right around me, I have seen more people out mowing and taking care of the yards of elderly people to help protect them from what could be deadly for them.

I have watched those I love suffer from this illness. But I have also seen concerned family, friends, neighbors, and even strangers, join in fasting, prayer, and love for those afflicted with the virus.

I have had a chance to do some of these things myself, and I have never felt a stronger sense of community, of belonging, and being part of something greater than my own small world.

And that sense of community has spread even wider, beyond those who live close together. I have watched on social media as people have sent out words of encouragement, songs of thanksgiving, and bits of humor to brighten someone's day, giving a feeling of oneness between us that often seems lost in today's world.

And all that I have seen and experienced gives me great hope in humanity, that despite the hardships of the current times, we will come out of this better and more united, with a true sense of community.

The Grain Drill

It's planting time in our rural community. Much of the grain is in, and some of it is up just enough that the fields have a beautiful green tinge to them. In the higher country, the grain is just getting planted, and in the valley, the potato planting is moving into high gear.

As with harvest, farmers often help each other or share equipment during planting. Dean, one of the older members of our community, told a story about just such a time.

Dean didn't have a big farm, but it was necessary to provide for his family. One year he had worked much of the spring trying to get his grain drill working. He would just get one thing fixed when something else would break down, sending him right back to the shop.

Dean could see the days going by, and the time for planting was coming to a close. He couldn't see any way his old planter was going to work, so he started asking around to see if anyone had a grain drill they could lend him.

The first farmer he asked had his grain drill up in the high country and wouldn't be done until after Dean needed it. The second farmer said his drill had broken down just as he was finishing his own planting. He said Dean could use it, but it would take some time to fix. And so it went with farmer after farmer. Each was willing to let Dean use their grain drill, but it wasn't currently ready or available.

Finally, Dean called Cyrus, who had a small farm, much like Dean's.

"Sure, you can use my grain drill," Cyrus said. "I don't even plan to use it this year. I have planted some hay, but I plan to put the rest of my fields into potatoes."

Dean asked if the grain drill was ready to go or if it needed work.

"Well," Cyrus said, "it was working when we parked it last spring. Of course, every spring, a person would do well to grease the bearings, oil the sprockets, and things like that. But that's all I think it should need."

Dean felt relieved. He met Cyrus at the shed by Cyrus's house where the grain drill was parked. Dean backed his pickup up to it as Cyrus directed him. They hitched the grain drill to Dean's pickup, and Dean was on his way.

When he got it back to his shop, Dean grabbed his grease gun and the oil can and started to freshen up the grain drill to ensure everything was working correctly. Before he kicked in the mechanisms to make sure everything was running, he opened the hopper to make sure there was no old grain or anything inside that might clog the drop chutes. He was surprised to find it full, but not of grain.

Dean called Cyrus. "I think you ought to come over here. There are some things in the grain drill."

"Like what?" Cyrus asked.

"I'm not sure what it all is," Dean said, "but I figure you should be the one to go through it."

It wasn't long before Cyrus's old Ford pulled into the yard. Cyrus got out, and the door squeaked like it would fall off. He walked over to Dean, who was standing by the grain drill. Cyrus opened the door on the hopper and stared intently, seemingly confused. He pulled out a bag.

Cyrus reached in the bag and pulled out a bunch of new blue jeans with the store tags on them. He still seemed confused. He pulled out another bag and pulled a doll out of it.

Cyrus's confused expression began to give way to a smile spreading across his face. "Oh, my diggity dang! That's where all that stuff went to."

"What is it?" Dean asked.

"When it's Christmas time," Cyrus said, "my kids have figured out all the hiding places we have for their presents. So, I decided to hide them where they would never find them. But the problem was, I couldn't remember where I put them, either. It ended up being a sparse Christmas."

Cyrus laughed as he gathered up the packages. "I guess my family is gonna' have Christmas in May."

Watering Greenhouses

With things opening back up a bit from the virus lock-down, I decided it was a good time to go to the nursery to get some flowers for my wife. She loves wave-petunias in hanging baskets around our deck.

I went to the nursery where my daughters used to work. Everyone was working feverishly to have everything in full bloom for Mother's Day. Most of them were busy watering. The water had a fertilizer mix that the plants loved, and it helped them grow quickly. A few were already in bloom, but others were still quite small.

As I watched the workers, I remembered a story my daughter, Heather, told me about one Saturday before Mother's Day. That day was always crazy, and for the employees, it was all hands on deck. I have gone there on those days and found no parking available in the parking lot, and I had to park out on the street.

The year Heather mentioned was an exceptionally busy one. The place was packed. Heather was assigned to water some greenhouses. But if a customer asked for help, that came first. Heather would hardly get any watering done between customers asking her to lift down the hanging baskets. Heather kept a pole nearby that had a hook on it. She could safely lower the desired basket to the waiting customer with it.

As soon as she would get back to watering, someone else would ask for a basket. The problem was that the greenhouses took hours to water, and it had to be completed even if she needed to stay after work. She had arrived before seven o'clock in the morning, and closing wasn't until eight o'clock at night. She hoped she wouldn't have to stay that late.

Then an emergency happened, ending the watering and all other activities. A mother started screaming that she couldn't find her five-year-old son. All employees were enlisted in the search. There was a canal on the far edge of the property, and some went to search there. Even some customers joined in the hunt for the little boy. But he was nowhere to be found.

All sales ground to a halt, and a huge line formed at the checkout. After searching everywhere they could think of that a small child might be, the owner designated two employees to continue the hunt while the others returned to their assigned tasks. Heather went back to watering.

She was watering a section of plants laid out in trays on tables built from pallets. The plants were dense in the trays and covered the area completely. As she was watering, she suddenly thought she heard a child crying. She turned around but could see no one, so she continued to water. But as she did, the crying grew louder.

Finally, she shut off her water and listened. The crying sounded like it was right beside her, but no one else was in the greenhouse. Then, suddenly, she had an idea. She knelt and looked under the table. There was a small boy hiding there. He was soaking wet and shivering.

Heather called another employee and informed her of what she had found. The employee left at a dead run and soon returned with the panicked mother. The mother came, knelt, and looked under the table.

"Timmy," she said, "what are you doing under there?"

"I'm hiding from you because you wouldn't buy me any candy."

No amount of coaxing from the mother could get the boy to come out, and the hole was too small for an adult to get through.

Eventually, the mother said, "Well, this young lady needs to keep watering. I'm going to have to let her do her job. I just hope the fertilizer in the water doesn't make your hair fall out or something."

And with that, the little boy came out from under the table.

Children

My last daughter moved off to college last week, and I already miss having children around. I work at home teaching, and like many of you, I don't go out a lot right now. But when I do, I like to observe the happy, positive outlook that children exhibit.

I was working in my garden when the three-year-old neighbor girl called to me. "What you doing?"

I stopped and wiped the sweat from my face. "I'm cleaning and pruning my grapes."

"What do you want to do that for?"

"If a person cleans, fertilizes, and prunes the grapes, they grow a lot better. And I really like grape juice." I then asked, "So what are you doing?"

"I'm helping my daddy build on our house."

"He is lucky to have someone like you to help him," I replied.

She nodded. "I know."

I thought about when I added on to our house. It was in the winter, and the temperatures were often close to zero. My little three-year-old daughter would get someone to dress her in her insulated coveralls, boots, and big mittens. Then she would come out and sit on the cement and tell me knock-knock jokes. Usually, she made them up on the spot, so they weren't all that funny. But she was cute and brightened my day as I worked, especially since she wanted to be with me. She is now twenty-two, but it seems like just yesterday.

Today, my wife asked me to stop and dig a few flower starts that a lady had offered to her. When I got there, a small boy, about nine-years-old, met me at my car.

"Is your mother home?" I asked.

He didn't answer the question but asked, "Are you here to dig some plants?"

"Yes," I replied.

"Then you don't need my mom. She's busy, so I will show you where they are."

He led me around to the plants in the backyard, and as I started to dig, he started to talk.

"My name is Daniel. I bet you're sick of this isolation thing. I know I sure am. I have lots of friends, but I don't get to see them because I'm not in school. . ."

A little girl that looked just like Daniel eventually joined us.

"This is Lizzy," Daniel said. "She doesn't go to school because she's only four. A few days ago, it was her birthday, and there was a big wind storm."

Lizzy nodded. "And I went out in the wind, and it blew me over, and I got hurt."

Daniel nodded. "Lizzy is the princess of owies. She's always getting hurt."

"When the wind hurt me, I cried," Lizzy said. "But when I went in the house, my mom said it wasn't that bad, so I didn't even get a Band-Aid."

"That's the sad thing about growing up," I said. "When you get hurt, you seldom get a Band-Aid, and when you do, they're never the fun kind with dinosaurs or ducks or something. They're just plain old brown Band-Aids."

"That doesn't sound like fun," Lizzy said. "I hope I don't ever grow up."

A little blond neighbor girl wandered over. "What are you doing?"

"I'm digging flower starts," I replied.

"Can I help?" she asked.

"I think you would get your pretty dress all dirty," I said. "I don't think your mother would like that."

"I'm sure she wouldn't mind," the little girl replied. "She sent me outside and said to have fun. And it's more fun if you get dirty."

I dug for a while, and they continued to talk. I enjoyed their take on life. When I finished, Daniel said, "Do you want to see the fort I made?"

We all trooped around the side of the house, with me trying to social distance from my new friends. Daniel had leaned the tree limbs that had broken off in the wind storm against the house. The girls loved it, and I praised him for being so innovative.

As I left, they waved, and Daniel called out, "Come back sometime, and you can play in the fort with us."

I smiled and thought, "I would like that."

True Happiness

As Steven climbed into his van, he thought a lot about Ben. Ben was slightly mentally slow, and some high school kids made fun of him. But Ben was always happy. No one ever saw him without a smile.

Steven had seen some senior boys make fun of Ben, and Ben just rolled with it. Steven could see the hurt in Ben's eyes, but his happy smile never faded. Steven was sure everyone liked Ben, even the boys who teased him. They just got caught up in the teenage group mentality.

Steven thought about a particular day in his English class. The assignment had two parts. They first had to write about what they liked, and then they had to write about what they would change if they could.

As the students started reading their papers, they were much the same. They liked their smartphones, their gaming systems, fancy cars, and expensive dates. What they would change was always others. They would change how this group or that person would act, how this teacher would grade, or how their parents would deal with them. After many of these, it was Ben's turn.

Ben struggled to read what he had written, and at first there were lots of snickers. But as he continued, the class grew quiet. Ben said he loved to rock his baby brother and feed him his bottle. Ben liked it when the baby fell asleep in his arms. He liked hot cookies fresh from the oven, rainbows, and sunrises and sunsets. He liked to see baby animals born in the spring. He liked Christmas lights and seeing the family gathered together on Christmas morning. Nothing in Ben's paper said anything about expensive presents, but everything was about family and the joy of life around him.

When Ben read his part about what he would change, a person could have heard a pin drop. Never once did he mention someone else. He said if he could, he would change himself. He would be a better son, a better brother, a better friend. He wished he could read and write better and be smarter. But the reasons he gave were not for his own benefit, but so he could be a help to others, especially his younger siblings. Never once did he mention that he wished others would treat him better, nor did he complain in any way.

Steven was called on next. After hearing what Ben had said, Steven was embarrassed about what was in his paper. Steven knew Ben's simple list was far more important in what really mattered. Steven couldn't even read his essay. He put it away and spoke from his heart. All who followed did the same, and Steven knew that Ben, in his simple way, had changed them all.

That night Steven went home and asked his mother if he could feed his baby sister her bottle. His mother looked surprised. Steven had always acted annoyed at having a noisy baby around the house, and indeed, he had been annoyed. But as he cuddled the sweet baby in his arms, and she smiled up at him, he felt closer to heaven than he had ever felt before.

Steven's thoughts came back to the present, and he watched all the other students climb into his van. When the van was packed with students, he drove them to his house. He went inside, and his mother handed him some hot cookies fresh from the oven. He and his friends then drove to the hospital. The same ailment that made Ben struggle mentally was taking his life. The group hoped to bring some cheer to him.

Ben greeted them with his usual smile. Other than the fact that he looked weak and pale, a person would not know his life was ending. He was happy, as always. He loved the warm cookies and insisted on sharing them with everyone. His happiness and laughter were contagious, and those who had come to bring Ben cheer found themselves the ones that were cheered.

Ben passed away the next day. The funeral was much like

Ben, full of happiness for the kind of life Ben had lived. His family didn't have a lot of money, and Ben's many friends donated to defray funeral costs. They also created a fund for the tombstone.

When Memorial Day came, Steven went to the cemetery specifically to see what had been written on the headstone. When Steven read what was written, he felt nothing could be more appropriate. It simply said, "He was always happy and made others feel happy too."

Needing a Reminder

Jennifer's children wanted a dog. That is normal for children, and Jennifer decided that maybe it would be good for them to learn responsibility. So Jennifer sat down with them and talked to them about how important it would be that the dogs were taken care of properly. Dogs needed to be fed at the same time each day. They needed to be taken for walks on schedule and trained with consistency. Her children agreed, so they all went to the animal shelter so each child could choose a dog.

Because they lived in an apartment, Jennifer insisted that the dogs not be too large. So her daughter got a medium-size dog, while her son chose a small dog. By the time they got home, the dogs already seemed to love their new owners, and the children loved their dogs.

As is usually the case, when they first got the dogs, the children took care of their pets without any reminders. But as time went on, the children forgot occasionally. Jennifer never did the feeding but would remind the children if they forgot. She was pleased that her children never complained when she reminded them, though she hoped it would become a habit for them to remember on their own.

Children, of course, grow up. And it seemed like no time at all before her daughter graduated from high school and was off to college. Jennifer's son was good to take over the feeding of his sister's pet. He seldom needed to be reminded to do it, and he did it when asked without hesitation. A couple more years passed, and Jennifer's son was also off to college.

That was when Jennifer found an interesting anomaly in her life. She had never forgotten to remind her children to feed the dogs. But now that it was her responsibility, she couldn't seem to remember for herself. More than once, she was tucked in her warm bed when she heard whimpering and realized she had forgotten to take care of the dogs.

Jennifer tried to think of ways to remember to feed the dogs on schedule. She would put something strange out of place, write a note and stick it on the fridge, or have her computer send her a reminder. But nothing seemed to be a permanent answer. Then she hit on an idea.

Jennifer's children had been encouraging her to get an Amazon Alexa. From what Jennifer had heard about that technology, it would be the perfect device for just such a task. So Jennifer ordered one, and it arrived a few days later. She immediately read through the instructions and set it up.

As soon as Jennifer figured the Alexa out, she set it to remind her to feed the dogs at five-thirty each evening. She arrived home from work at about four-thirty, so that gave her time to get settled in first.

The dogs also got used to it. When Jennifer got home, they became excited. They settled down for the next hour, but the dogs would get eager just before Alexa announced it was time to feed them. When the announcement came from Alexa, the dogs would come tearing through the house to find Jennifer. The funny thing was, Jennifer hadn't realized until then that when she had reminded her children, the dogs had immediately run to the children. It was just more pronounced with Alexa.

The routine went on for almost a year, then the covidvirus hit. All normalcy in Jennifer's schedule went out the window. Jennifer worked from home, and everything seemed turned upside down. Days just ran together. She was especially grateful then for Alexa's reminder to feed the dogs.

But one day, having worked inside much of the day, Jennifer decided to take a walk. She wasn't thinking about it being late in the afternoon. She just felt the need to get out. When she came home, she found the dogs had made a horrible wreck of the house. They had never done that before. Why did they do it now? That was when she realized it was after six o'clock, and she had been gone for over an hour. Alexa had obviously announced it was time for their feeding, and the dogs had torn the place apart trying to find her.

Maybe using Alexa to remind her to feed the dogs wasn't such a good idea after all.

It's About Community

(Part 1)

I put the phone down and let out a sigh. Donna, my wife, asked, "What's wrong?"

"That's the fifth number I called that said the phone number is no longer in service."

She nodded. "I've had the same problem. It seems that everyone is switching to cell phones. I heard that in the future, a person will be able to make their landline number their cell phone number. Then it won't be a problem."

"Well, right now, I need some help getting the Flinders' water pipes unfrozen. They're too old to do it themselves, and I don't have the equipment I need."

Eventually, I was able to get the help I needed. Still, the delay made me think about how the inability to contact each other was affecting our little community. I decided to do something about it. I was going to create a directory.

I approached the community and church leaders about the idea. They had experienced problems like mine and were all in on the plan. The church leaders even said I could send a list around in church. Everyone was supportive except for one man. When I announced what I was doing, he became outraged.

"That is totally illegal to collect people's information," he said.

"It is not illegal if they choose to give the information, and I don't use it for commercial purposes," I replied. "A person can share their phone numbers and emails if they choose or withhold them if they want. And I plan to make it clear on the directory that it is not for commercial purposes."

"Well, I'm not giving you my information," he said belligerently.

"That's fine," I replied. "But I don't feel it is proper to share information with anyone who is not on the list."

He was the only one who didn't put his name on the list. But the next day, he appeared at my door. "Here's my info, and a ten-dollar donation to help with the printing. I want the first copy. I wasted over an hour trying to get hold of someone today who had changed their number."

I put together the list with the numbers I had, but more than half of the community did not go to the church I attended. There were about 150 families in our community, so I still had a lot of work to do. I decided to take a couple of hours right after church each Sunday and visit the rest of the families. With people wanting to talk, and others not being home when I stopped by, it took longer than I expected.

When I pulled up at the home of one new, young family, I could see the husband busy chopping wood. His three children, who were eight, six, and five, were struggling to carry the pieces of wood to the shed to stack them. The pile of wood to be stacked was large and growing faster than the children could move it.

I took off my suit coat and tie. "Can I help?" I asked.

The surprise showed on the young man's face. "Uh, yeah, I guess so."

We worked for a couple of hours, and, with my help, the children and I finished stacking at about the same time their father finished chopping.

The father invited me to join them for some lemonade, which I gratefully accepted. As we sat down to visit, he introduced himself as Brent and his wife as Wendy.

When I explained the reason for my visit, Brent looked shocked. "You helped us stack wood for a couple of hours, dressed in your suit, and all you want is our phone number and email for a community directory?"

"But we're not members of your church," Wendy said.

"This is a community directory," I said, "not a church one. We all try to help each other."

"What will you use the information for?" Brent asked.

"Mostly, we'll use it to be able to get hold of each other. As for the email, my wife has volunteered to send information to a list I will set up for her about things like when people have lost a pet, have garden produce to give away, need help, or things like that."

"That's really strange," Wendy said. "In the place where I grew up, I didn't even know my neighbors' names."

Wendy looked at Brent questioningly, and he nodded. She turned back to me and smiled. "We'll share ours, and I think it is going to be interesting to be part of a community like this."

It's About Community

(Part 2)

In the process of trying to put together a community directory, I had stopped and helped a young family get their wood for winter stacked in their shed. When I talked about how the community helped each other, the wife, Wendy, was surprised. But as Donna, my wife, used the email list I set up to share information about lost pets, cows out on the road, and extra produce, Wendy seemed to enjoy being part of it. But she still seemed timid about being too involved.

Then at five o'clock one Saturday morning in February, I got a call from Wendy. "Mr. Howard, you talked about the community helping each other. Well, I need some help, and I don't know who else to call."

Wendy said their wood supply had been running low. Her husband was a trucker and had taken a load to South Dakota. He said he'd be back before the wood ran out, and then he'd get them more.

"But he got caught in a snowstorm in Wyoming," Wendy said. "He's not back, and we're out of wood. My family's really cold, and I don't know what to do."

"I'll be over as soon as I can get some wood loaded in my pickup," I replied.

I quickly dressed. On the way out the door, I asked Donna to call the community leaders and tell them about the situation. Because of the snow, I had to pull loads of wood from my shed out to the road on a sled. It took most of an hour to get a full pickup load.

I parked by their house and started to haul armloads of wood inside. Wendy's eight-year-old daughter joined me while Wendy started a fire. By the time we finished carrying the wood in, the fire was burning, and the children were gathered around the woodstove.

"You and your children would be welcome to come over to our house," I said. "It is nice and warm."

Wendy smiled. "Thanks. But I think we'll be okay now."

When I got home, Donna met me at the door. "The men and boys have already organized to cut and chop a load of wood from the community stockpile. Grab some quick breakfast, and then you can join them."

I ate quickly and hurried to the community woodpile. This was a stack of wood we had piled up from dead trees we had hauled there in the fall from along the canals. The chainsaws were buzzing, and the axes were flying. I joined in chopping. The young boys teased me about being so old, but with my specialized ax that never gets jammed, I was soon outpacing them. The boys started begging to try my ax, and I was relegated to stacking wood on the trailer.

It wasn't long before we had the big trailer filled. Some men and boys went home. But since Wendy knew me better than the others, the community leaders asked me if I would direct the group that would deliver the load of wood.

"Sure," I said. "I'd be glad to."

As we backed the trailer into the driveway, I could see Wendy's children peeking at us from between the window curtains. When we started stacking the wood in the shed, Wendy came out.

"What's all this?" she asked

"That little load of wood I brought won't be sufficient for you," I said. "So the men and boys in the community got together to get you a load of wood that would get you through the winter."

As we finished stacking, filling the shed to overflowing, Wendy started to cry. "I've never experienced anything like this before."

I smiled. "When you live here, you are part of us. And to us, it's all about community and taking care of each other."

It's About Community

(Part 3)

Wendy had grown to enjoy the friendliness and care our small community members had for each other. When her husband, Brent, was caught away in a snowstorm, Wendy was amazed to see the men and boys in our community come together to get her the wood she needed for her family to stay warm. But there was even more to come.

I was one of the first ones to meet with Brent and Wendy when they first moved in. I had been putting together a community directory at the time. For that reason, I was usually the first one Wendy called when she needed help. It was no different this time. It was around four o'clock in the morning when the phone rang, and I groggily answered it.

"Mr. Howard," Wendy said, her voice sounding terrified, "my house is on fire, Brent is on a long-haul trip, and we need help."

I immediately snapped wide awake. "I'll be right there."

As I ran to get dressed, I told Donna, my wife, to call the fire department and others in the community. It took me less than a minute to dress, throw on a coat, and head out the door. But by the time I had driven the mile to Wendy's house, other men were already there. I found out later that a neighbor had gotten up to use the bathroom and had seen the fire. He immediately started calling people.

The fire was in the chimney and the attic. Three men were already passing buckets of water up to douse the flames in the attic. But they would just get it out in one area when it would burst into flames in another. Wendy and her children were still in pajamas. I got them into my warm, idling van, then rushed inside to shut down the woodstove. With a towel wrapped around my hand, I helped another man shut all the air vents on it. Once the fire started to die down in the stove, the fire in the attic and chimney were brought under control.

By the time the last embers were fading, the place was swarming with people. The fire department arrived and took over, making sure all traces of the fire were out. Men, women, and teenagers carried what could be salvaged out of the house. I had lived in some big cities, and a fire like this, and the image of people carrying things off, would have made me think of less-than-honorable intentions. But none of that was even a worry here. Though everyone was loading the stuff in their cars, it was only to take the items and store them out of the weather until it they could be returned.

When everything had settled down, I drove Wendy and her family to my home. My children were just getting out of bed, and they helped Donna find clothes for Wendy and her children. We all had breakfast, and then I had to go to work.

By that evening, when I came home, I found out that the people of the community had gotten together and fixed up a house for Brent and Wendy's family. The house hadn't been rented in about six months and needed some repair. A whole crew of the retired men, directed by some old carpenters, worked all day on it. They had just called and said it was ready.

Wendy and her children loaded into our van with my wife and me, and we drove to the house. The men had done a great job. They had even brought over what was useable from the burned house. People were coming and unloading the stuff from their cars they took out of the house earlier. At one point, I heard Wendy tell a lady the blankets she was bringing in weren't hers.

"They are now," the lady said. "The ones I took out of your house were filled with smoke. If I can wash the smoke out of them, I will bring them back, too."

Much of the evening was like that. Besides bringing back items salvaged from Wendy's burned house, people brought many things of their own that they thought Wendy could use.

Donna and I were last to leave, and as we turned to go, Wendy smiled, and with tears in her eyes, said, "It really is all about community and helping each other, isn't it?"

A Happy Dog

My two-year-old granddaughter, Hannah, loves animals. When she comes to our house and I take her for a walk, we have to stop and pet every cat or dog that she sees. Hannah especially loves to go out in the backyard and pet our golden retrievers. They stand as high on all fours as Hannah is tall, and she can look them right in the eyes.

One of Hannah's favorite things to do is to feed the dogs treats. I have taught my dogs to sit and not move when I hold out a treat. Then I toss the treats in the air, and the dogs jump for them. Since Hannah can't throw very far, I hold her in my arms when I let her feed the dogs. I am afraid that she won't throw it far enough away from her, and she might get knocked down.

Besides loving animals, Hannah is very smart. It's hard to hide Easter or Christmas candy and not have her find it. More than once, she has had the telltale sweets smeared all over her face and clothes.

When you put Hannah's love for animals together with her ability to get into things, you have an interesting combination. That's why I wasn't surprised when my daughter-in-law, Janalyn, told me what Hannah had done on a visit to Janalyn's sister.

The sister had a small dog. It was a frisky little thing that jumped and danced around everyone's feet. It was friendly, and everyone loved it. But no one loved it more than Hannah. She would follow it around and play with it.

At one point, Janalyn's sister pulled a large jar out of the cupboard, took an item out of it, and dropped it in the dog's bowl. The dog immediately wolfed it down and begged for more. But the jar was put back into the cupboard, and Janalyn's sister went on to other things.

The family had dinner and then sat around visiting. Now and then, Janalyn would see Hannah drop one of the items into the dog's food dish and watch the dog gobble it down. Janalyn thought it was sweet of her sister to let Hannah feed the dog so many treats. Most people would only give one or two snacks to a pet in a day, but Hannah had been doing it all afternoon.

The dog, for his part, was enjoying the attention. Whenever Hannah would approach its food dish, it would dash over there expectantly. The dog seemed so happy to have Hannah around. In fact, Hannah's attention to it seemed to make the dog more and more excited.

"Your dog really likes Hannah," Janalyn said to her sister.

The sister smiled. "He does, doesn't he? It's probably because Hannah is more his size, and she gives him so much attention."

"He sure gets excited around her," Janalyn said.

"True that," the sister said. "Usually we just ignore him, and he settles down and is quiet. He's old, and his energy subsides quickly. I guess with someone to play with, he has more energy."

Janalyn nodded. "And it's nice of you to let Hannah feed him those doggy treats, too."

This time the sister stared at her. "I don't have any doggy treats."

"But didn't you feed him a treat when we first came?"

The sister laughed. "No, I just fed him a. . ."

Suddenly, the sister's face went white. She jumped up and ran for the kitchen with Janalyn close behind. There, sitting on the floor, was the big jar Janalyn thought was the treats. It was now almost empty.

"You didn't give Hannah those to feed your dog?" Janalyn asked.

The sister shook her head. Looking around and seeing a chair pulled up next to the counter, it was easy to see Hannah had retrieved them herself.

"If they aren't doggy treats," Janalyn asked, "then what are they?"

"That was a bottle of one-hundred-and-fifty hemp pills. The vet gave me a prescription for them, and I just filled it yesterday."

"Oh, no!" Janalyn said. "Will your dog be okay?"

The sister nodded. "It's a low dose, just enough to give him a little energy. But with all of them, it might be a while before he winds down."

They put the pills away, but for the rest of the day, they had one very energetic, happy, slightly loopy dog.

Teaching Scouts
(Part 1)

One of my scouts came into camp, shaking his head. "You know that troop next to us? I don't think they know anything."

"What do you mean?" I asked.

"Oh, I don't know," my scout replied. "It's just everything about them. They're over there trying to build a fire, and I think about the only thing they're going to burn is themselves."

"Maybe I should pay them a visit," I said.

I wandered down the trail. The other troop wasn't really right next to us. My boys liked to be as far out from the center of camp as possible and always got the last camp on the edge of the forest service land. We had two unoccupied camps between the next troop and us.

As I stepped into the other troop's camp, I could see what my scout was talking about. In the fire circle they had big logs. The scoutmaster, along with a few other boys, were down on their knees trying to light the big logs on fire with matches. The matches kept burning out long before the log caught on fire. A couple of the boys lit paper, but it quickly burned up while only singeing the logs.

I walked right up to the group. "Hi. I'm from the camp farther up the trail."

The scoutmaster stood, smiled, and spoke somewhat coolly. "Aren't you the group that never wears scout uniforms?"

I smiled and nodded. "That would be us."

I looked around the group gathered there. The scoutmaster and every boy had on a perfectly ironed scout uniform.

The scoutmaster smirked and said, "Don't you think it's strange that you're the only troop not wearing scout uniforms at scout camp?"

"Not really," I said. "To me, scouting is about skills more than it is about ceremony." I then pointed at their pile of singed logs. "Been camping much?"

The smirk disappeared from his face as he shook his head. "No. We live deep in the city, and it's impossible to find any place to camp without driving for hours. That's why the boys have been looking forward to this one."

"Mind if I take a shot at your fire?" I asked.

The scoutmaster shrugged. "Go ahead and try. But be forewarned, I think we must have defective wood."

I asked them if they had a hatchet or an ax, but they didn't. I asked one of the boys to grab me some paper towels. I pulled out my knife and took one of the roughest logs. I whittled off some shavings and long splinters. Once I had a good pile, I put the paper towels in a pile, then piled on the small pieces of wood. I also directed the boys to bring me small branches and pine needles from the surrounding forest. I broke the branches and laid them with the pine needles on top. Soon I had a good pile. Finally, I placed three of their big logs in a triangle against each other over the other wood.

I lit the paper, and almost immediately, the whole pile started to burn. Soon the big logs caught fire, and it wasn't long before a roaring fire was blazing in the fire ring.

"Well, I'll be," the scoutmaster said. "I thought something was wrong with our wood."

"You've got to start out small and build it up," I said. "I suppose we all have our talents. I wouldn't know much about living in a city. My boys and I aren't much at wearing uniforms. But we do a lot with survival skills."

I held out my hand. "The name is Daris."

He smiled a much friendlier smile. "Steven," he replied.

"If you need anything, you know where I am," I said.

Steven nodded. "If I do, I will definitely come find you."

Teaching Scouts
(Part 2)

Steven, the scoutmaster of a new troop at scout camp, had a lot to learn about scouting. It's true, at the campfire program where all the troops gathered for the evening program, his troop always wore top-notch uniforms. My boys seldom wore anything besides jeans and t-shirts. When the camp directors yelled, "Who's got spirit!" Steven's troop yelled the loudest. My boys sat there quietly, looking disgusted.

One night, after Steven's troop won the spirit stick for the second night in a row, Steven came over to me.

"Your boys don't seem to have any Scout spirit at all."

I smiled. "Oh, my boys have Scout spirit. They just don't think yelling has anything to do with scouting. But you wait until the conclave games on Friday. I will put my boys up against any troop in lashing, bridge building, fire starting, or anything you want. That's what scout spirit is to them."

"But don't you want to win the spirit stick?" Steven asked. "You've got the biggest troop and could win."

I shook my head. "These boys are farm boys that spend their days working hard. When I became their scoutmaster, we compromised on certain rules. I wouldn't make them yell for the spirit stick, and I wouldn't make them wear uniforms except to important ceremonies and when doing anything with flags."

"Whatever you're doing with them must work," Steven said. "When I go around to the different merit badge stations, the top boys on the list are always from your troop. I keep wondering what your camp is like."

"If you ever want to drop by, feel free," I said.

The next day, at dinner time, Steven came. I invited him to join us for dinner, and he accepted. Most of the boys were doing their assigned chores.

"How do you get them to do their part?" Steven asked. "My boys whine about everything."

Just then, Mort came over. "Daris, do I really have to haul water tonight?"

"Of course not," I replied. "I'm on the kitchen cleanup. You can do that, and I'll haul water."

"I'll haul water," he said, rolling his eyes and picking up the water cooler on his way to the nearest spigot.

I turned back to Steven. "I always work with the boys. I willingly join the group doing the job they hate the most. That way they can't say I expect too much of them, and I always can offer to trade."

We had a decently good spaghetti dinner—decent by scout-cooking standards. Then the boys wanted to play Old Sow. I was visiting with Steven, and Gordy brought me my stick. "Come on, Daris. We challenge you to be the sow tonight and see if you can get the puck into the center again."

I quickly explained the rules to Steven. Each boy had his stick in a hole on the perimeter of a large circle. Everyone was against each other, and if a boy pulled his stick out of his hole to whack the puck, another boy could steal that hole, leaving the first boy scrambling for safety. Until I came along, the boys had always stolen each other's holes, sending the one without one off to be the sow and get the puck. But I played differently. When I played, I took the puck through all the striking sticks into the hole in the center of the circle. That was the ultimate win.

I left Steven to join the boys. I started bringing in the puck, which was just a block of wood. Soon sticks were flying as each boy tried to knock it out for me to chase. Two or three times, the puck was sent flying, and the boys laughed as I chased it. But eventually, expertly blocking their sticks and maneuvering the piece of wood, I got it into the center circle and stood on it.

"I win!" I yelled, as the boys groaned and demanded a rematch the next night.

As I came back, Steven smiled. "I think I'll go teach my boys to play Old Sow."

I smiled. "Be careful. Until you get good at it, you probably don't want to try for the win."

As Steven left, Mort asked, "Do you think his troop playing Old Sow is a good thing?"

I laughed. "I guess we'll see."

And the next day, we did see. When Steven came to the campfire program, he had bruises all over him and some stitches over his eyebrow.

Mort elbowed me and pointed at Steven. "I think you forgot to tell him the rule about the end of the stick having to stay below the knee."

Teaching Scouts
(Part 3)

Because the boys in my troop liked to stay at the farthest camp out in the woods, it wasn't uncommon for us to have problems with bears wandering into our camp. One night a bear came in search of food. Rod, my assistant, ran to the main lodge and got some pepper spray we could use to drive the bear out. We kept it with us all the time after that.

One evening, as our troop was sitting down to eat, we heard growling, screaming, and the most tumultuous noise come from the camp closest to ours. Before we could do anything, Steven, the scoutmaster from that camp, came running to us.

"There's a bear tearing our camp apart!" Rod and I both pulled out our pepper spray and jumped up to help, but then Steven continued. "The boys dragged an orphan cub into our camp and tied it up."

Both Rod and I stopped and turned to Steven. "You tied a cub in your camp?" I said.

Steven nodded and spoke fearfully. "The boys found it and said they were sure it was orphaned. They felt sorry for it, brought it back to camp, and tied it there so they could feed it. That must have made some bear mad."

"Not just some bear," I said. "That its mother. Sometimes mother bears leave their cubs to forage. I'm sure she traced the scent to your camp."

"Pepper spray might not drive off an angry mother bear," Rod said.

I nodded. "We just need to make sure everyone stays out of there until the bear can free her cub." I then turned to the boys in our troop. "Mort, David, you two take the south trail to stay away from the camp. Run back to the lodge and inform the camp leaders.

Gordy, Devin, and Dallin, you follow me around to the north of the camp to warn anyone coming from that side. I will defend against the bear there. Rod will drive the bear away if it comes this direction. The rest of you go down the south trails, warn anyone coming from that direction, and do whatever Rod tells you. Make sure no one goes near that camp!"

I took the three boys I assigned to work with me, and with Steven following close behind, we cut out through the woods to the west to swing wide around Steven's camp. I sent each of the three boys north along different trails to warn anyone who might come from that direction. I got as close to Steven's camp as I dared and stayed there. From that point, I could hear the bear growling, ripping, and smashing anything she could.

I turned to Steven. "You did get all of your boys out of there, didn't you?"

He nodded. "Everyone ran when the bear came." Then, with his face as white as ash, he asked, "What will you do if she comes at us?"

"We're not standing here to fight her," I said. "If she comes, you run, and I will try to deter her from coming down into the other camps. I don't think she will because she will probably stay close to her cub until she can get him free. What was the cub tied with?"

"Just a bunch of rope," Steven replied.

"Hopefully, after she takes out her anger on your camp, she will rip through the rope, take her cub, and leave."

After a while, the smashing stopped, and the growling faded away. I was sure the mother bear and cub were gone, but I wanted to give them plenty of time, so I waited. When the camp directors showed up, I explained the situation.

We cautiously made our way into the camp. The bears were gone, every tent was torn to shreds, and benches and tables were overturned. Almost nothing was left untouched.

The camp directors were upset. One of them turned to

Steven.

"Mr. Dickson, you, your assistant, and the boys in your troop need to meet with us at the lodge right now!"

Steven nodded. "Yes, sir. I will find them, and we will be there." The camp directors left, and Steven turned to me. "Hey, thanks for taking charge. I was at a loss as to what to do."

I shrugged and smiled. "I bear-ly did anything."

Steven only smiled slightly. Maybe it wasn't a good time for a joke.

Teaching Scouts
(Part4 - Final)

Because Steven, a scoutmaster from another troop, had let his boys tie up what they thought was an orphaned bear cub, their troop got in big trouble. After its mother tore up their camp, they were summoned to a meeting. My troop had just finished eating when Steven came by.

"How did it go?" I asked.

He shrugged. "They asked us to leave because they said we endangered all the troops here. It's probably for the best anyway. The bear tore apart everything we have, so there are no tents or sleeping bags."

"I'll come help you," I said.

As we walked along, I could tell he was discouraged. When we got to their camp, I joined in the cleanup. It was a big job. Many of my young men voluntarily came to help, as did others. As we worked, Steven expressed his love for scouting and how he had looked forward to being a scoutmaster.

"But I guess I'm just not cut out for it," he said.

"I think you're wrong," I replied. "You have the three main things it takes. You love the boys, you're willing to learn, and you know you're not perfect. With your willingness to learn, you're going to be a great scoutmaster."

He looked at me briefly, then spoke with new resolve. "Would it be okay if I came back tomorrow and watched your boys compete in the conclave games? If I'm going to learn, I should start right away."

"We'd love to have you join us," I said.

The next evening, Steven showed up just as our troop was finishing dinner. We offered him some food, and he settled on a plate of Dutch oven cobbler.

I gathered the boys around. "We have a big troop and have been allowed to form two teams."

I then assigned the teams with a team leader and members according to abilities. I chose the best two fire builders and put one on each team. I did the same with the bridge-building and other events. I tried to keep the teams as equal as possible. I told them the boy I assigned for each event was in charge of that event, and the others were to help him and follow his direction. Rod, my assistant, went with one group, and I went with the other. Steven came with me. It was fun to watch my boys excel at most of the events.

Steven expressed his amazement. "Your boys are incredible. How did they get so good?"

"It's important to know your weaknesses and strengths," I replied. "I teach them where I am strong, I have Rod teach where he has more expertise, and I'm not afraid to ask someone else if needed."

"How do you get them to behave so well?" Steven asked.

"You remember how I told you my boys set their own rules under my direction? That's critical. It's hard for them to complain if they had a hand in setting the rules."

Just then, Gordy came running up. "Daris, we need you."

I ran after him and soon found myself at a wrestling challenge. A large, muscular boy stood there.

"I've beaten everyone who has challenged me all summer," he bragged. "Boys and leaders."

I turned to Gordy. "I don't think this is a good idea."

The muscular boy smirked. "It's worth team points. But we all understand. You're old and out of shape."

I handed Gordy my water bottle. "I think we could use some more team points."

It was three falls out of five. The muscular boy's smile faded when, after the whistle, I deftly picked him up in a fireman's carry and laid him on his back.

"I bet you can't do that again," the boy said.

On the second time, he shot in, I blocked him, pushed his head down, spun behind him, and locked a death grip around his waist until he could hardly breathe. When I put him on the mat, he panted, "I think two is enough."

As we gathered for the awards, the other troops yelled to show spirit, and my boys rolled their eyes and were quiet. But when the awards were announced, my troop won both first and second in almost every event. We also had the only points for the wrestling challenge.

When I came back from getting the wrestling-challenge award, Steven smiled. "I think the main thing I learned this week is that there's a lot more to learn about being a scoutmaster than what comes from a book."

Being Treated Right

Jan worked at a fast-food restaurant. Most of the workers were like her—college students with very little money, trying to make ends meet. She didn't mind the long hours and hard work. Most of the other employees were kind, and they got along well. But there was one thing that she really hated. It was when a customer came along who acted like she, or one of her coworkers, was nothing because they had to work at this type of job.

The worst person was a man who went by the name of Guy. Jan knew that wasn't his real name. He was a state politician and felt that made him privileged. Jan had seen Guy's impatience when the line was long. Even though they were moving food through quickly, Guy still felt it was the worker's fault when he had to wait more than a couple of minutes.

Jan knew she wasn't the only one who dreaded dealing with Guy. The minute he came in the door, everyone immediately found something to do so they wouldn't have to take his order. But this time, when Guy came in, Jan was the only one on ordering, and she knew she would have to deal with him.

To make matters worse, there was a new manager. Word was that Tess had been a manager in a tough, inner-city restaurant and had transferred here to go to school. So, Jan was sure Tess had never met Guy before. Managers experienced with Guy would not take his negative remarks about an employee seriously. But a new manager might, and she might put that in the employee file.

Guy came to the ordering counter. Even though her heart was trembling, Jan put on her best smile and asked, "What can I get for you?"

Guy ordered, and Jan read the order back to him. True to form, he was annoyed.

"Can't you people get anything right? I ordered a large fry."

Jan knew for sure he hadn't, but she punched it in. She again read it back to him. He rolled his eyes and spoke in a loud, demeaning voice.

"Are you stupid or something? You didn't mark extra ketchup like I said."

Guy then proceeded to berate Jan, saying that her uselessness was why she worked there and would never work anywhere else. Jan knew Guy had said nothing about ketchup. She tried to speak, to tell him she would correct it, but her voice wouldn't work. She could feel her emotions getting the best of her as she tried not to cry.

Suddenly, Tess was by Jan's side. She looked at Guy and said, "What did you call her?"

Guy unashamedly said, "I said she was stupid and couldn't get the order right. And that she would never do anything but a worthless job like this. If it weren't for people like me, people like you wouldn't even have a job."

"You've got that wrong, mister," Tess said. "If there weren't people like us serving food and doing this kind of work, there wouldn't be people like you. And furthermore, we don't have to take your abuse. You can just go somewhere else to eat."

Guy was furious. "I want to talk to your manager!"

"I am the manger!" Tess replied. "And you can just take your hoity-toity attitude and leave! And if you get hungry, you can just chew on your better-than-others feelings until you get full of yourself, which shouldn't take long, because you appear to be mostly there already!"

Guy glared at Tess, but Tess met his glare with one of her own and didn't back down, even though she was half his age. But then something else happened. Another regular customer, who had seen this play out with Guy many times, stood and began to clap for Tess. Others in the restaurant joined him.

If there was one thing that could change the attitude of someone like Guy, it was community disapproval. When he saw how others felt about his treatment of Jan, he looked like he could crawl into a hole in the floor. When the clapping died down, Guy even apologized. Then he asked, "May I please still order?"

Tess nodded to Jan, and Jan finished the order without another word from Guy.

And Jan knew that she and Tess were going to be best friends.

Sandy

There are world-famous sand dunes near where we live. Though they are about a mile away, on Labor Day and Memorial Day weekends the amount of noise late into the night is so loud we have to close our windows to get some sleep.

I never take my family there on those weekends. The hills look like giant ant colonies, with every ant riding a four-wheeler. We don't ride all-terrain vehicles (ATVs), and even though there are rules about those who do staying away from others, a person takes their life in their hands to be out there at those times. It reminds me of when I tried to cross the streets of New York at rush hour.

But on weeks outside of holidays, and on a weekday and not on a weekend, I might take my family out there to play on the sands. The children liked to run and jump off the hills, flying down the steep embankment until they landed in a soft sand cloud.

On one such outing, we had been out there all evening and were on our way back home. The children were tired and were sipping ice water. They were looking forward to popsicles at home, another family tradition. But on the way home, my youngest daughter, Elli, suddenly called out to me.

"Dad, look. It's a small kitten, and it's alone."

As we drove by, I caught a glimpse of the kitten in the field.

"Please," Elli said. "Can we go back and get it?"

"Sweetie, it's probably wild," I said. "Either it would run away if you tried to get close, or it would claw at you."

"But it looks abandoned and afraid," Elli replied.

Elli has a big heart, and I knew that if we didn't go back and check on the kitten, she would worry about it. I also knew that sometimes people who tire of their pets drive into the countryside and leave them. These animals, not knowing how to fend for themselves, usually starve or grow mean and are killed. I turned the van around, and we went back.

When we stopped, the kitten cried loudly at us. I didn't know if it was crying for help or as a threat, so when Elli approached the kitten, I stood by in case it turned on her.

Elli walked slowly toward the kitten, and suddenly it ran at her. I had seen even small animals that were wild and vicious, so I ran to protect Elli. But the kitten clawed its way up her pants, and before I got there, it had climbed into Elli's arms and buried its frightened head into the crook of her arm. Elli petted it, and it kept its head against her as it continued its sad cry.

Once in the van, the other children wanted to see it, but it kept itself tightly in its position of safety. When we got home, I got my first close look at it. It was tiny, skin and bones, and its coat was mangy. It must have been out there for some time. I was surprised a coyote hadn't gotten it.

Elli named the kitten Sandy because we found her on the way back from the sandhills. We gave Sandy some milk, and she devoured it. But she was so near starvation that she immediately threw it up. We struggled to save her. For more than a week, we fed her many times per day, but only small amounts. She often still couldn't keep the food down. But finally, she was eating full meals and having no problem.

But then we had another complication. Our other cats, all drop-offs like Sandy, refused to accept her. Though it was sad for Elli, we convinced her that Sandy would do better in another home. So, Donna, my wife, found a lady looking for a kitten companion.

Elli, Donna, and I took Sandy to meet the lady. The lady immediately fell in love with her. Though it was hard for Elli to say goodbye, we promised she could come back and visit. A few months later, we did take Elli back. Sandy was a beautiful, sleek, playful juvenile cat. She immediately seemed to recognize Elli and climbed into her lap, curled up, and purred herself to sleep.

And as Elli petted Sandy, we all knew we had done the right thing in going back to rescue a lonely, lost kitten.

A Fair Deal

Ken took his seven-year-old grandson, David, to the fair. It was a big fair, and there were lots of things to see and do. There were the animal barns, the homemaking displays, and, of course, the carnival rides. Both Ken and David loved the big draft horses. David enjoyed the fancy chicken breeds, while Ken felt they were somewhat useless. But when it came to the rides, Ken was not so keen on them at all.

"Come on, Grandpa," David said. "Let's go on the big Ferris wheel."

That didn't even sound fun to Ken, especially since they had just eaten. First off, he was afraid of heights, and second, he could envision himself throwing up on all the people below.

"Well, what if I go, and you just wait for me?" David said.

Ken shook his head. "I know how young people are. A person can't trust them out of their sight for an instant. They do things they shouldn't do, acting like daredevils and risking their necks. You're not going on it alone, and I'm not inclined to go with you."

Ken suggested that instead they should try their hand at throwing the balls at the pins in one booth. David was disappointed, but he agreed to that. A little while later, with twenty dollars less and a toy a person could buy for a dime, they gave up on that activity.

"Hey, look, Grandpa," David said. "How about the octopus ride? That one doesn't go too high."

Ken asked the ride operator, and the ride operator assured him that none of the chairs went more than ten feet off the ground. Ken decided that was a ride they could take.

Ken paid the money, and he and David got themselves buckled into one of the chairs. But what Ken quickly learned when the ride started was that it didn't just go in a circle like a merry-go-round. Each chair also spun around. By the time the ride finally came to a stop, Ken was not only feeling nauseous, but he desperately needed to find a bathroom.

They hurried around the fairgrounds to the bathroom building and found a line snaking back and forth among chains for about fifty yards. Ken considered the situation and then knew what to do. They had been at the fair for a long time, and it was pretty much time to go home.

David balked at leaving, but he was good to do what he was told, and soon they had walked back to their car. Ken knew he couldn't make it all the way home, so he stopped at the first place he found that he knew would have a bathroom—a Walmart.

Ken rushed in as fast as possible without garnering too much attention, keeping David in tow. When they got to the bathrooms, Ken dropped David's hand.

"You stay right here, and I'll be back in a minute," Ken said.

He hurried into the bathroom and located an empty stall. Soon he was feeling much better. But when he stepped out, to his horror, two women were standing there washing their hands. That was when he realized he must have gone into the wrong bathroom.

One woman started screaming when she saw Ken. She also yelled for security, and everything Ken did just made it worse. Then, suddenly, David appeared.

David came over and took Ken by the hand. "Come on, Grandpa, we need to get you back home."

The lady stopped screaming and spoke kindly to David. "This is your grandpa?"

David nodded. "I'm so sorry about the problem. You know how old people are. A person can't trust them out of their sight for an instant. They do things they shouldn't do. I'll take him out of here now."

The lady smiled. "You are a good grandson."

The fact that David had used Ken's own words didn't go unnoticed by Ken. And once David had led Ken by the hand out of the store, Ken stopped and looked at his grandson.

"You know, David, I think you're responsible enough to ride the Ferris wheel on your own. Let's go back to the fair and let you ride."

And that's just what they did.

The Water Boy Wrestler

(Part 1)

When February rolls around, that month when wrestling and basketball are coming to a close, I often find my mind slipping back to my athletic days in high school. I recently found myself reminiscing about the first high school wrestling tournament I ever participated in. It was a Junior Varsity tournament. Our small school had a J.V. wrestler for every weight except heavyweight. Thus, with eleven wrestlers, one water boy, and our coach, we headed to a nearby town for an all-day tournament.

We nicknamed our water boy Curly, or Sheep, because of his tightly curled hair, and he definitely was not a wrestler. But he had the two qualities needed in a good water boy: he could carry water, and he could tell stories better than anyone. When we returned from our wrestling meets, he would twist the most mundane match, where we were facing a very inferior opponent, into a tale where it sounded like we were going up against an agitated Godzilla and coming out conquerors.

His persona was that of a giant marshmallow. His physique was the same. When Coach approached us from the meeting where they determined the ordering of the wrestlers in the tournament, he was excited. "Curly," he said, "no other team has a heavyweight, so I am putting you in, and you can win team points for us by default."

"But, Coach," Curly protested, "I don't have a wrestling uniform."

"No problem," Coach said. He turned to me. "Howard, you're the next biggest wrestler. You will have to hurry to the locker room and switch your uniform to Curly."

"But, Coach," Curly complained, "it will be all sweaty."

"Besides," I added, "my wrestling uniform is half the size of Curly."

"What a bunch of whiners," Coach retorted. "I could open a distillery as much as you guys whine. A little sweat won't hurt you, Curly. And Howard, you find a way to stuff him into that suit if it kills you."

There was no arguing with Coach, so after my first match, I ran for the locker room. Coach had already sent Curly there, and he was undressed and waiting. I flew out of my uniform, and we started pulling it up around him. It took Frank, Lenny, and me, along with Curly, to stuff him into it. We were tugging the uniform and poking parts of him in, like trying to squeeze a king-size pillow into a couch-cushion pillowcase. We finally got most of him in the uniform, but he was still sticking out all over. The uniform looked like someone had painted it on, and it wasn't a very good paint job.

As I scurried into my other clothes, Curly started to complain. "I can't move in this thing. If I do, I'm sure I'll tear something."

"You better not!" I said.

"I meant me!" he grunted.

"Just take little, itty bitty steps," Lenny, our 98-pound wrestler, suggested.

"I'm not walking out there like a stupid ballerina," Curly argued.

Just then, the second call for Curly came on the intercom. A third call, and he would be disqualified. Suddenly, Coach appeared and bellowed like a bull, and Curly minced his way out of the locker room with us behind him. As Curly walked gingerly onto the mat to have his hand raised for the default win, the crowd roared with laughter.

The following two rounds went similarly. After each round, I could feel my uniform getting looser. In the late evening, when the two lines were formed for the final championship match opponents to shake hands, something interesting happened. A huge heavyweight wrestler, somewhere close to the size of a Mack truck and looking like a Neanderthal, lined up across from Curly. He was from the host team, and as such, had not had to appear for his default hand-raising.

Curly became frightened. He turned to Coach and pointed at the other wrestler. "I'm not going to wrestle him!"

Whether Coach knew all along there was another heavyweight wrestler, we will never know, but he was absolutely defiant. "You wrestle him and die like a man, or I'll take care of you myself!"

The Water Boy Wrestler
(Part 2)

✧

Coach had put our marshmallowish water boy, whom we called Curly, or Sheep, because of his hair, in to wrestle, claiming there were no other heavyweight wrestlers. Coach said Curly could win us team points by default. He had no uniform of his own, so we had to stuff him into mine each time. Then, at the championship round, we found there was a huge, ape-size heavyweight from the home team. Curly was frightened, but Coach told Curly he would wrestle and die like a man if he had to.

The evening wore on, with our team taking a large share of the championships. As I stepped out to wrestle in my now-saggy, stretched uniform, Coach turned to Curly. "Curly, run in and get ready to put on Howard's. . ." But Curly wasn't there. "Where in tarnation did Curly go?!" Coach thundered at us.

"I think he's hiding," Frank volunteered.

"Well, get him found!" Coach yelled. "Howard, you get out on the mat and wrestle your match. The rest of you spread out and find Curly."

While I wrestled, ten other wrestlers ran frantically in every direction. As I stepped off the mat at the end of my match, Frank came running up, panting. "Coach, we found him. He's locked himself in the bathroom in the dressing room."

"Oh, for crying out loud!" Coach gasped. "Howard, get in there, get that uniform on him, and get him out here before I do something I will regret!"

I ran for the locker room and slipped out of my uniform. I could hear Lenny trying to coax Curly out of the bathroom. "Sheep," he said, "what's the problem, man?"

"I want to live to be older than 15," Curly wailed from

behind the locked door.

"You've got to do it, man," Lenny prodded, "or Coach is going to make you walk home."

"At least I'll be alive," Curly retorted.

By this time, I was dressed in my regular clothes, and I tried to help. "Curly, my friend, you may not be alive if Coach catches you. They've already done the first call, and if they call you again, Coach will be coming in here." All was quiet in the bathroom, so I continued. "Just go out there and keep away from him."

"Keep away from him?!" Curly almost bawled. "I can't even move in your stupid small wrestling suit. How am I going to keep away from him?"

Frank came flying into the dressing room. "Coach is coming!"

At the mention of Coach, the bathroom door popped open, and Curly ran to the uniform. We joined him and started poking pieces of him into it as Coach crashed into the room. "What in heaven's name is taking so long?!"

"The uniform's wet and tight from sweat," I replied.

"Well, get a move on!" Coach thundered as he headed back out to the gym.

We barely arrived back in the gym, with Curly in tow, as the third call came. Curly, both timidly and gingerly, stepped onto the mat, taking tiny steps as my wrestling suit, stretched like a rubber band, fought to stay in one piece. Curly's opponent took his position on the opposite side of the circle. They shook hands, and we all held our breath as the referee blew his whistle.

The shrill sound of the whistle hadn't even faded before Curly was running for the edge of the mat like a ballerina in a hundred-yard dash. It was obvious he was racing straight for the bleachers, but he didn't get that far. Just as he made the boundary of the circle, Mr. Mack Truck made a dive and caught Curly by the ankles, tripping him and plopping him, bouncing, onto his soft underbelly on the edge of the mat. Mack then started to drag Curly back toward the center circle.

Curly, in desperation, grabbed the edge of the mat and held on for dear life, popping all the tape that held it down, and rolling it toward the center. The ref, who was gasping with laughter, sounding like he had swallowed his whistle, was trying to find enough air to blow it. Finally, a tiny squeak came out. The crowd's laughter nearly drowned it out, but the two wrestlers were finally separated. The ref, still red-faced from trying to hold his laughter inside, pointed to Curly and called, "Warning! Stalling!"

"I wasn't stalling," Curly yelled at him. "I was running as fast as I could in this stupid suit!"

The clock showed that only ten seconds had passed of the first two-minute round. It was going to be a long match.

The Water Boy Wrestler

(Part 3)

Coach had put our marshmallow water boy, Curly, in to wrestle, claiming there were no other heavyweights. Coach said Curly could win team points by default. We stuffed him into my uniform each time, and it was so tight that he walked like a ballerina. Then, at the championship round, we found out there was a huge Mack-truck-size heavyweight from the home team.

After Curly ran for his life at the first whistle, Mack had caught him at the edge of the mat and dragged him back to the center. Curly had grabbed hold of the edge of the mat, rolling it up as he went. As we all helped unroll the mat and tape it back down, Curly quietly asked me, "Howard, how many stalling warnings do you get before you are disqualified."

"You get two warnings with no point loss," I replied. "Then, on the third and fourth times, you lose points. It isn't until the fifth time that you are disqualified."

"Five times!" Curly hollered. "I've got to go through this four more times to be disqualified!"

We got the mat taped down, and the referee lined up Curly and Mack. Now the whole crowd was watching with great anticipation, grinning, and holding their breath as the ref blew his whistle. Curly jumped the whistle with an incredible burst of speed, the likes of which I had never seen him demonstrate before. Even running in small ballerina-type steps because of the tight wrestling suit, he almost made it to the bleachers. But then Mack dove and caught Curly's ankles. Curly flopped onto his belly on the hardwood floor right by our team bench. Curly grabbed desperately for anything he could. Unfortunately for Lenny, he was within grabbing distance. Curly latched onto Lenny's ankles, pulling Lenny off the bench onto the floor as Mack pulled Curly back to the mat.

The ref was choking so hard he couldn't blow his whistle to call them out of bounds, so Mack kept dragging Curly, who was dragging Lenny, back to the center circle. Lenny was desperately trying to pull free of Curly's grasp, and the palms of Lenny's hands were sliding, squealing across the wood floor.

Lenny's kicking was wriggling him out of Curly's grasp, and, as they reached the edge of the mat, Curly let go of Lenny and again grabbed the edge of the mat. Once more, the mat started to roll toward the center. The ref, who could hardly breathe, let alone blow a whistle, started waving his arms like he was driving crows off a grain field. Finally, Mack stopped dragging Curly, and Curly stopped dragging the mat.

The ref took some time to catch his breath, and when he had, he could barely be heard over the laughter of the crowd as he pointed at Curly and chortled, "Stalling! Second warning!"

"Only the second one!" Curly yelled. "I can't run any faster. Can't we just skip to the fifth one and call it good?"

The ref was perplexed. No one had ever asked for extra penalties before. He didn't know what to say, so he simply said, "I can't. It's against the rules."

Coach, his face now red from embarrassment, wasn't sure what to do. Coach was the only one not laughing besides Curly, Mack, and Lenny with his scraped-up hands. As we unrolled the mat again, Coach grabbed Curly by the arm. "Why don't you just pin yourself or something for crying out loud?! It couldn't be worse!"

Coach, of course, was speaking figuratively, but Curly thought he was serious. To make matters worse, Curly apparently thought it was a good idea. After the mat was again secured, the ref lined the two opponents on opposite sides of the circle, and, even though the laughter of the crowd had not totally subsided, he blew the whistle.

And Curly set out to do just what Coach suggested: to get himself pinned to end this match.

The Water Boy Wrestler

(Part 4 - final)

Coach had put Curly, our marshmallow water boy, in to wrestle, claiming there were no other heavyweights. Coach said Curly could win team points by default. We stuffed Curly into my uniform each time, and it was so tight he walked like a ballerina. Then, at the championship round, we found out there was a Mack-truck-size heavyweight from the home team.

After Curly ran for his life twice, only to be dragged back to the center by Mack, Coach was embarrassed and facetiously suggested to Curly that he should just pin himself. Curly apparently thought that was a good idea.

The two wrestlers again lined up across from each other. The instant the whistle blew, Curly flopped on his belly, then rolled onto his back, arms outstretched, right in front of Mack. Mack was confused. He looked like a deer caught in the headlights. He looked at Curly on the mat, then at the ref, then back at Curly, then back at the ref. The ref, who had overheard Coach's suggestion to Curly, was gasping and choking. His face was red, and his whole body shook as a gurgling came from his throat. Coach was yelling at Curly to get up. But Curly lay there as Mack continued to stare, unsure what to do.

The ref's inability to blow the whistle caused the time on the clock to run out for the first round. As the buzzer sounded, Curly still lay there. Finally, the ref, not knowing what else to do, got enough air to blow his whistle and pointed at Curly, who was still lying in the center circle. "Third stalling!" Then, pointing at Mack, the ref raised two fingers. "Two points."

Curly could hardly get off his back. He was like a turtle flipped over. To make matters worse, the wrestling suit kept stretching and popping as he tried to rock onto his stomach. Finally, he rolled over and struggled his way to his feet. He got right up in the ref's face. "What are you talking about? I wasn't stalling. I got on my back as fast as I could. I was pinned, and you know it. I demand you call a pin."

The tears were now flowing down the ref's face. He obviously had never had anyone demand he call a pin against them before. It probably went against all the rules he knew. He shook his head. "I can't call a pin if your opponent isn't on you."

"But I was flat on my back!" Curly argued.

"I'm sorry," the ref retorted. "It wasn't a pin."

I heard an old man sitting behind our bench say, "This is the best entertainment I've had in years. I would have paid $50 to see this show."

The coin was tossed, and Mack won the toss. For a second, he almost took the down position, but then it seemed to occur to him that if Curly was on top, he would probably run, and it would end up being another chase. So Mack took the top position. The ref signaled for quiet, and finally the crowd simmered down. Curly knelt, gasping for air as the suit cut off his breathing.

Mack got on top and put his arm around Curly. The ref blew his whistle, and Curly rolled so fast onto his back that he rolled right out from under Mack, who dropped flat on his stomach. As Mack scrambled to his knees, Curly, realizing he had rolled too far, started trying to scoot himself back over to Mack.

As Mack knelt there, staring at Curly inching his way back over, Curly's voice suddenly rang out through the gym. "Get over here and pin me, you moron!"

Mack, finally coming to himself, jumped toward Curly, landing on him with a thud. Curly let out a grunt and yelled, "Not so hard, you idiot!"

With both Mack and Curly trying to move Curly into a pin position, they seemed to be working against each other, and neither could get Curly's shoulders flat on the mat. Finally, the ref, apparently having a feeling of mercy come over his heart, and desperately needing to stop laughing so he could get some air, slapped the mat, ending Curly's torment.

From under Mack, Curly's voice sounded loudly. "It's about time!"

Mack kindly helped Curly to his feet.

The crowd cheered and clapped. "Never seen anything like it in my life," the old man behind us chortled to his friend.

As the heavyweights took the medal stand, and Curly was announced for his second-place medal, the crowd rose and gave him the only standing ovation I have ever seen at a wrestling tournament, especially for the person who lost.

Deep-Fried Twinkies

When my nephew, Brandon, first brought Hannah to our house, we all loved her immediately. The two of them were going to school at the nearby university, and they joined our other nieces and nephews who were going to school there in coming out for dinner. Hannah was from Kentucky and had a bit of a Southern accent. She told us that she came from a unique family. Her father's family are engineers, doctors, and lawyers.

"But my mother's family are what people would call Rednecks," she said. "Both families are wonderful, and we'd all get together at our house for holidays."

"How did they get along?" I asked.

"They all thought the other family was strange," she replied. "But they did seem to like each other. That's why they kept organizing family gatherings together."

Hannah showed both parts of her heritage in her personality. I saw in her a lot of her father's love for learning. But it was one Thanksgiving Day when I first saw her mother's side.

By then, Brandon and Hannah had gotten married. We invited them and all my other nieces and nephews out for Thanksgiving dinner. When Hannah walked in, she was carrying a pecan pie. Hannah made one of the best pecan pies a person ever tasted. She set it on the table and turned to me.

"Are you having turkey?" she asked.

I nodded. "It's in the oven."

She paused and looked at me with disbelief. "It's in the oven? You mean you're not making a deep-fried turkey?"

"No," I replied. "I'm cooking it in the oven. I've never had deep-fried turkey."

"Well, I've never had a Thanksgiving turkey cooked in an oven," she said. "We always had our Thanksgiving turkeys deep-fried."

"I'd like to try that sometime," I told her. "I bought an extra one for another day. Maybe you can teach me how to deep fry it."

"I don't know how to deep fry it. That was always Uncle Bubba Bob's job. He said the secret was in the marinating sauce injected into it, and he never shared that secret with anyone."

A couple of months later, when it was my wife's birthday, Brandon and Hannah came for dinner again. I was making my usual Twinkie cake. I first made it when my wife and I were engaged. It was my only option after I destroyed three cakes in attempting to bake one for her. The Twinkie cake consisted of Twinkies stacked in a pan, frosted with whipped cream, and decorated with M&M'S. I thought it was impossible to lose with that combination, and it was a big hit with everyone. Everyone, that is, except for Hannah.

"What are you making?" she asked when she came into the kitchen.

"A Twinkie cake," I replied.

"What's a Twinkie?"

I couldn't believe she had never had one before, but after visiting with her, I found out she truly hadn't.

"I don't think they have those out where I live," she said.

I tossed her one from the stack. "Here. Try that."

She unwrapped it and took a bite. She got a horrified look on her face. She ran to the sink and spit it out and washed out her mouth.

"How can you stand that thing?" she asked. "It was all sweet and gushy and everything. That has got to be the most disgusting thing I've ever put in my mouth."

I laughed. "Why, because it wasn't deep-fried?"

"That might have helped it," she said, "but I'm not sure."

I made some brownies for Hannah, and we often laughed at our differences after that. But someday, I want to try deep-fried turkey. And maybe both Hannah and I will try deep-fried Twinkies.

If you enjoyed this book, please leave a review on Amazon at:

https://www.amazon.com/dp/1629860247

Would you like to see the Life's Outtakes column running in your local paper or magazine? Suggest it to the editor. If an editor runs the Life's Outtakes column due to your suggestion, we will send you a free autographed book by Daris Howard. Find out more here:

http://www.darishoward.com

Read stories, purchase books, or subscribe to our short story list by going to

http://www.publishinginspiration.com

Daris Howard's Amazon page:

http://amzn.com/e/B004H76UGK

For inspiring plays and books, as well as discounts for booksellers, go to

http://www.publishinginspiration.com

About the Author

Daris Howard, an award-winning author and playwright, grew up on an Idaho farm. He was a state champion athlete, competed in college athletics, and lived for a time in New York.

Daris has worked as a cowboy, as a mechanic, in farming, and in the timber industry. He is now a college professor. He has also been a scoutmaster, having up to eighteen boys in his scout troop at a time. In his wide range of experience, he has associated with many colorful characters who form a basis for his writing. Daris has had plays translated into German and French, and his plays have been performed in many countries around the world. For many years, Daris has written the popular column Life's Outtakes, which consists of weekly short stories and is published in various newspapers and magazines in the US and Canada.

www.ingramcontent.com/pod-product-compliance
Lightning Source LLC
Chambersburg PA
CBHW050737230626
47052CB00002BA/468